THE LOST AND THE FOUND

Tales of the Civil War in Virginia and
how love and respect can help
overcome adversity.

Told in three stories

Volume Two About the Civil War

Ellen Murphy

BOOK I - My Son Is Missing!

Chapter One

Henry Thomas had finally finished the farm chores for the morning. His farm wasn't very large compared to some but complete, in that it had orchards for apples and peaches; also, he was trying some Bartlett pears now. He had several kinds of grain, mostly wheat, which was the best seller, but also rye and oats. He had a large field each of soybeans, and tobacco (which only did marginally well for the weather wasn't warm enough this far north). He had a large field of feeding corn with a lesser field of sweet corn. He had done well with it before the war but he was exhausted now with Jamie, his son, and three other helpers in the army – all but one Confederates. The other, Bobby Lance, had gone back to his home in Maryland, where his parents insisted he join the northern army, so he was a Yankee.

Henry sauntered slowly back to the house with "Hunter", his bloodhound close to his heels, wondering how he would ever reap the harvest this year...several retired farm workers would help - friends of Carl who worked a lot for the Johnsons but would help him as well. No use worrying about it. He would pick and run the horse with various apparatus as he could. There were two nice families of blacks who would help, but both also worked for the farms where their houses were located. None of them were slaves. He would think on his proposed ideas over his dinner. As he walked, he talked to the dog – may as well – no one else to talk to. He was too sad to make any attempt at conversation with a neighbor.

He had been notified that Jamie had been killed at the battle of Gettysburg. His wonderful Jamie! This year of 1863 had been hell! Bright and friendly and just a very, very good boy! What a waste! A loveable and responsible kid. He had joined the Confederate Army, feeling he had a responsibility to keep things under their own control and not by orders given by someone who didn't live in Virginia. Some of this had been prompted by Yankees coming onto their land and trying to take the black workers back to "freedom" in Pennsylvania. What nonsense! None of them were slaves here. He knew that was done elsewhere but not here. All the blacks he knew of and had met were free working people, with their own houses and church and everything!

Well, so much for that! Every so often now, at least every few days, but sometimes weekly he would have a visit by Jamey's betrothed, Charlotte Johnson. As much as Henry loved her and wanted to see her, he sincerely hoped she would find someone else to make her life whole, someone else to love. She had come regularly since Jamie joined the army but now she was in bad shape as was he with the reported killing of their special person. He had hoped it was a mistake, but the letter had identified him by name and rank. He didn't want to believe it nor did she, but the paper was plain as day and signed by two Yankee officers.

Charlotte and Jamie had liked each other a lot since grade school and become engaged when he left for the army. But that was over and she should move on. He would have loved to have her for a daughter-in-law. She would have made him feel blessed...but life has to go ahead, just as he has to tend the animals and continue working the farm, she should move to a future where she could have some enjoyment. She was really beautiful, not just in looks – which she was, but in her attitude and work ethic, intelligence and sweetness! Just about perfect! She would always come and help them with gathering produce and picking fruit. She loved to climb trees! Not exactly considered a lady-like activity but she would laugh off any admonishment and climb as high as any man and pick as much fruit too.

The Johnson's had a farm that was huge by current Virginia standards and was operated very well by her father with considerable help from his family and the many people they hired. Workers were available for them, including two dark families, NOT slaves, few in this area had ever OWNED anyone else. Most dark workers had their own residences, churches and were paid. Their properties maintained by the farm owners. They also had about six other men who worked the farm...did have eight but two of the younger went to war. The overseer was Tom Hicks, who had worked for Johnson for years and years. He was gray-headed but spritely and worked many hours – seeming to enjoy it. His wife kept house for him and their three daughters were all married and gone to homes of their own – but not too far away.

Johnson was a spectacular man and his wife Helen too. He would send his workers to help Henry harvest or do repairs and adamantly refuse any recompense. But not only to his but to other small farms in the area, like Howard England's parents, or the Reids and the Martins. Just as God would wish, Mr. Johnson would say.

There had been no gardening done by Henry today. He had overdone it yesterday with weeding, hoeing, picking and so forth. He was tired and he was hungry! While doing all this pondering, Henry and Hunter had made it back to the house and he definitely knew it was supper time. My he was hungry, the small sandwich he had made did not last long. He opened the ice box and there on the block of ice was the left-over dinner from last night (and the night before but who's counting?) He had made a baked chicken dish with potatoes, onions and peas in a creamy gravy. It had a biscuit topping, too. Using the large crockery baking dish – therefore enough for at least the three meals. Instead of heating just a portion of it tonight, he put the whole dish with the rest of it in the oven.

The wood stove had continued to stay warm with some coals and now he stirred the firebox about and added some wood. Henry put down some food and water for Hunter. He took a minute to empty the water in the melted ice pan under the ice box, into the slop bucket, before going upstairs. Then he went into his room to take off his shirt and wash his face and hands. He patted the side of the bed where his Carole Ann had always slept. He hadn't worked hard today, just the normal. Fed the chickens and gave them clean straw, fed the pigs. Next came the horses, brushing them and checking on their feed and water. He milked the remaining cow and fed it, plus shoveled out it's stall. There was no gardening to do today. Not for the first time did he consider getting another younger cow and a bull – but didn't have the energy or enthusiasm now with Jamie gone.

Coming back downstairs after he cleaned himself up, combed his gray hair and put on another shirt the stove was indeed again roaring and the oven hot enough that the chicken supper was bubbling. The biscuits would be a little hard but he had added some milk and water to soften the gravy and the biscuits would be all right when crumbled up in that.　He rummaged in the kitchen "safe". Not like a bank safe but a large cupboard with perforated metal panels in the sides for air circulation.　It was used for holding jars of fruits and preserves, cakes or pies, and such things as one might need when cooking - like crocks of salt and spices. The perforated panels were quite decorative in the sides but only had very tiny holes and would not let mice or flies in.　He found what he needed: a jar of damson preserves that Carole Ann had made three years ago.　He looked at the paraffin top and saw it was intact, as Carole Ann had always shown him, so it was still good…Yes! His favorite. There were four jars left of the damson.　He kept the damson bushes trimmed, maybe he could find a kind woman at church that would make him some damson preserves. With a whole row of bushes there would be enough to share with the maker and he could provide the sugar too.　However, he imagined he could do it himself when his ran out, although he hadn't tried. I bet I can, he thought – he had helped often enough. His donation of fresh damsons to the Johnsons and Reynolds the last two years had been appreciated. Making preserves wasn't as hard as making a cake. Preserves were only a few ingredients.

He had over-done work yesterday, with weeding, hoeing, picking and so forth. His back had reminded him last night!

He heard Hunter woof and then woof again. Must be someone about but without the loud barking Hunter could do, it most likely was someone they knew.

Sure, and certain, with her buggy tied to the hitching post there came Doris Rogers! What in tarnation had brought her all this way? It was at least an hour from her house to his. He didn't know if his dinner would stretch to two but he could open a jar or two of vegetables he supposed. Plus, he still had several jars of peaches.

Opening the door before she could knock, he realized he had startled her. "Well, Doris, come in. I am sorry if I scared you but Hunter told me someone was here. Come in!"

"Oh, I forgot that Hunter would alert you. I apologize for coming unannounced, but I had visited the Johnson's to see if Helen was better. When someone has a cough I always worry. But she is fine. She gave credit to the homemade brandy you had sent by Charlotte. What a dear girl! And Helen said to thank you again. If you don't mind, when you have a chance, can you write down how you make it? I have never made spirits but everyone says your brandy is the best!"

"Well, I don't know about that, but I will look up the recipe in Carole Ann's box and see what I find. I don't quite remember all the steps off the top of my head – I always had to look. It has been a very long time since any was made here. Of course, it keeps forever. Would you like another bottle, I should have at least half a dozen left?"

"Yes, if you can. That would be very nice. Again, I apologize for just dropping by. I do have a plate of those blueberry scones you like as a peace offering."

"I can provide you with some supper, in return for the scones. It isn't much and was made a couple days ago. However, it has been on ice and is reheating as we speak. I'm not the cook Carole Ann was but it isn't too bad, if you would like some?" While they talked he opened two jars of green beans and put them on top of a shredded strip of frying cured ham.

"Well, although invited, I didn't eat at the Johnson's but since it is ready, if I join you I should still make it home before dark. That is a "Yes" if you wondered!" and she laughed.

"Very good! Here I'll put some fresh warm water in the bowl for your hands and set the table for two." Emptying the little bit of remaining water in the wash bowl into the slop bucket, he refilled the bowl and handed her a clean towel.

"Hunter! Back! That dog, he thinks everyone wants to pet him. Oh, I see you are…well no wonder he crowded you. Isn't he something! But he keeps me from talking to myself most days. Such a good dog and quite a watch dog too. He only woofed a little when you drove up so I knew it was a friend but when it is a stranger you can hear him all the way to Little North Mountain I believe!"

"I have never replaced, Tracer, my Tom's old dog. but I think it may be a good idea. A way to alert me to someone coming near the house. Of course, Mable is still living with me, but the dog would probably hear anyone before either she or I did. I'm certain she would appreciate a dog. She always spoiled Tracer."

"Yes, most assuredly, it would be good to have a dog. Although you are not real isolated on the edge of town, still if it became known only two ladies lived there you might be bothered by some 'ner'do'well. Some of the army deserters are a problem. Josh, with the store at the Springs, has some pups ready for homes.

They are nice spaniels and therefore have a good disposition. Perhaps you should look at them and see if any takes your fancy," he said as he stirred the beans.

"Oh, what a good idea. I shall do that! Mable would be so happy. She has been a dog lover all her life. I am not as familiar with the beasts except for our old one who was really Tom's but I realize it would indeed be a good alarm to have such a pet!"

At that time, she looked down and Hunter was sitting beside her looking expectantly at her. "Oh, I believe your dog would like another pet. Look at him sitting here. Isn't he soft! Well look, he's turning his head for some more petting! I believe I will like a dog – at least if it is one a nice as yours!"

"The pups should be of a similar disposition. Most dogs, when part of a family, are quite nice. They get used to protecting those they live with. The only I know who aren't like that are those in kennels all the time on farms where they are used for hunting. I have heard of guard dogs – used to protect property or a person…people have been training such for centuries. Dogs as a rule are protective of those who care for them and those they love. I have never trained one so – never taught a dog. I better get a move on; I shall have our supper ready in a couple minutes. What would you like to drink? I have water hot for tea and I have cider cooled in the ice box, or I believe two lemons left and could make lemonade…"

"Oh, hot tea would be nice, thank you. I don't need cream. I hope I am not putting you to a lot of trouble. But Mable doesn't eat an evening meal – she snacks a lot during the daytime. So, this way I won't have to eat by myself."

"Well, here it is. Just chicken and biscuits but I have green beans with ham and peaches too."

"How nice this is! I dread eating by myself and sometimes Mabel can be enticed to sit with me, particularly if we invite the gentleman next door. I think he is sweet on her. Henry, this is delicious. You do all your own cooking?"

"For the most part. Sometimes Charlotte Johnson will bring something her mother has made. But rarely. I don't want to encourage her very much. She needs to get over her heart break about Jamie and find another nice young man. But she doesn't seem interested in doing that, so I don't say anything now. She will do what she must I guess. But a lovely child, she is that!"

"So many on the battlefields have been misidentified, are you quite certain Jamie was killed?"

"I assume so. I guess I really don't know for certain. Just what I have been told. None of us identified him or anything. I wouldn't wish such a loss on my worst enemy but would be thankful to my dying day if it wasn't he, but I have tried to just accept the notice I was given."

"Thank you so much for the delicious dinner! And those peaches were divine. Did you can those?"

"No those are left from a couple years ago but I will do so this year. My supply is getting low and I know how to do them. Some things are more complicated but I can do various canned fruits. Heavens to Betsy, your scones are divine. Blueberry is my very favorite flavor! Thank you! I will keep some for breakfast with my coffee. Coffee is so hard to come by with all the blockades, that I make do with tea except in the morning. It takes the stronger coffee to get this old body moving anymore."

"I hate to eat and run but if I leave now I won't have to rely on the lanterns on the buggy to see where the road is. Thank you for the dinner it was delicious and the peach pie heavenly. Just as an aside, and I know I am overstepping, but maybe you should look about Jamie and be certain he is indeed lost to you...I know that is impertinent of me, but with the shooting over in Gettysburg, maybe you should go up and look in the hospitals."

The following morning, as Henry again reflected on what Doris had said yesterday about Jamie, he thought perhaps he was not diligent enough. If Charlotte would come by he would talk it over with her. He had no one here to watch the place and travel with him but maybe Charlotte's father would spare a man to go if they needed and maybe Old Carl could stay here with the dog, feed the animals, milk the cow and collect the eggs, or generally look over things. No one knew just how old Carl was – not even Carl - but he was an old man when Henry was a boy. However, he still lived on the Johnson property and often did help others during harvest or canning or even at the store at the Springs. Quite a remarkable old fellow! The more he thought about it the more he wanted to actually look things over up there in Pennsylvania. No fighting was being done now, that he knew of, so he would probably be safe with the war almost over. If Jamie's sweet girl came by tomorrow he would talk to her about his making a trip to Gettysburg.

After another day of exhaustive work, as he crawled in bed, tired again, he reflected on how nice and pretty Doris was. So energetic, he had missed the activity about the house when his wife was alive. Hunter seemed to really like her and although someone not familiar with dogs wouldn't understand, it was a fact that dogs were a good judge of character. Proof of that was the way the dog got so excited when Charlotte came.

As he finally got relaxed enough to sleep the last thing he pictured was Jamie grinning at him from the top of an apple tree with Charlotte beside him – both picking fruit and putting it into their canvas sacks.

It would be nice to have someone to go with him if he traveled to Gettysburg. A long and lonesome trip by himself to see to such an awful possible outcome! But then again maybe not so awful – maybe wonderful: what if Jamie was ALIVE? Finally, he dozed.

Chapter Two

As he walked back to the house the next day, from all his morning errands, including gathering the dozen eggs, milking the cow and snipping off some vegetables, he was hailed by Tom Evans.

"Well, for Heaven's Sake, Tom, how are you?"

"I am fine now, Mr. Thomas. All healed up. I can't raise my shoulder properly but I can still outrun you if you want to race your buggy again!"

"Ha! So, you are feeling your oats, are you? Well, bring it on! Oh, it is good to see you up and around. I am so pleased you took the time to come in my lane. I bet your parents are elated. How is your Dad, what happened with his leg?"

"Well, unfortunately the doctor did have to remove it below the knee to save the half leg. It was just too shattered by the mini-ball to repair and was looking a bit infected, Doc Pritchard did some surgery and Dad came through it with no problem. He has been fitted with a stump that doesn't hurt his knee too badly and using his cane can get around quite well. He asked that I give his greeting to you and tell you to plan to come by for a couple days soon. He and I were fortunate enough, I guess, to be injured near home. Better than at Gettysburg or to the south!"

"I have been reflecting on Jamie. The more I think about it, and Doris Rogers agrees, I should go up and check the hospitals and so forth...rather than take their word for it. What if he lost his paper and someone else had it, what if he is lying in a bed somewhere? I really feel I need to check. I was hoping Charlotte or her father would be by today and I could discuss it with them."

"I suggest you do so. The sooner the better. Having been in such a place myself, although far smaller than the many injured at Gettysburg, it is not carefully done. My nurse was forever calling me Tom, when that is not part of my name at all and I had my papers – so without them, I guess my folks would have not been notified but some parents of a "Tom" would have! It is good seeing you, Sir. I need to get to the store at the pond for a couple things the general store at Stephens City didn't have like some more canning jars and lids. I'm glad I got to see you and when you finish your trip to Gettysburg, don't be a stranger. Come up the Pike anytime and Mother said we will put you up for the night – no need to make it a havey-skavey trip all in one day!"

"Thank you, Boy! Thank you. I will let you know. You be careful – no racing that carriage now!" and laughing waved good-bye.

It was early times yet, he wasn't hungry, why wait for Charlotte to come here? He would go to them. He hadn't visited the Johnson's in a long time and would enjoy seeing everyone. After banking the fire, letting the dog out for a bit, and gathering a bottle of brandy and a jar of pickles, he felt he was ready to head to the Johnson farm. With such an important issue to discuss, he had put the dog back in the house, changed his shirt, gabbed a weather-all jacket of oiled tight sail-cloth and headed out.

It would take him almost an hour, but the road was good and he didn't want to hurry the horse too much. He noticed the Smyth property was in excellent shape. The three families of darkies that they employed certainly took good care of the place. He waved to Tom as he drove past. He would stop another time and look at those two colts. He probably didn't need another horse but they were splendid. He would enjoy training a horse again, he certainly had the time.

Shortly thereafter he was driving his horse up the wide lane to Charlotte's home. Someone he couldn't identify had run into the house, when they saw him coming. Well, good, they could start this awful conversation right away. How was he to tell them, and particularly Charlotte why he was here? He hated to admit he couldn't accept reality, but he just had to check, now that he had decided there was no turning back. Go he would, as awful as it was bound to be!

Just as he tied his horse, Charlotte came running out of the house, smiling and greeting him warmly. "What's wrong, Pap, why are you here?" He loved it when she called him that, just like Jamie used to!

"Nothing is wrong, Sweet girl, I just need to talk to your father a bit. I am going to go to Gettysburg. I have procrastinated enough. I need to see things for myself!"

"Well, for Heaven's Sake, that is just what Papa said not an hour ago! Come on in and you can talk to him. He had the notion we should check on the hospitals there and be certain Jamie isn't lying injured in one. He had the boys clean up the big carriage and curry the two best drafting horses. Come in here and talk to him! Maybe it is an omen that you have both had the same idea! I am very afraid it is because of me. I just won't talk about the possibility of Jamie not coming back. I just can't. I guess I'll have to if he is in a grave but in my heart he is not!"

"Henry, come in. We have been talking about you and your son. It is quite timely that you have shown up! Jordan, take Mr. Thomas' things out of his buggy and put them on the porch, then please take his horse and buggy and put them up comfortably in the second barn. I believe he and I have a trip and we will use my carriage."

"Henry, Sir, are you too tired to make the long trip this evening. It would be quite late when we get there but I do have a room available in Gettysburg for us – to use what little of the night is left by then. My carriage has four big lanterns and I have additional lights if needed. Would you be comfortable enough to get on the way? Hattie has packed us considerable food and drink for the trip and if you are going I do not need to take Jordan with me."

"That sounds exactly right to me, Timothy. Let's go. Charlotte, angel, don't you worry about us. We will be fine and if Jamie is there, trust we will find him! Please find Carl and ask him to keep check on my house. He knows where the extra key is and can milk, collect eggs and feed the dog."

"I will be glad to do that for as much as I would love to go, I feel you will make better time with a lighter load for the horses and not as crowded to sleep. But know my thoughts and love go with you!" and crying she went back in the house.

As much as the horses were good and strong, it was the very devil of a trip and already morning before they got to

Gettysburg and contacted the man, whose name had been given to Timothy Johnson. They had encountered the river out of banks in Frederick, Maryland. Some Amish traffic further into Pennsylvania, and then a road closure because of damage from transporting cannon and other army issues. Once they found the man that had been recommended to make inquiries about injured soldiers, they found he was cooperative and said he would start the investigation. He would search by name while they grabbed a little breakfast or rather lunch and a nap. He would return with news for a proposed further plan for investigation later in the day. They agreed and went to Mrs. Hubbard's boarding house where their room was arranged. She was a cousin of the Lodge's at White Hall and had been informed he may be there for a room while searching for news of his son.

As tired as they were they couldn't help but be pleased with Mrs. Hubbard's kindness. She provided hot beverages, scones and a variety of meats, and had used bed warmers with hot coals so their feet would get back to normal. Both had on sturdy boots and wool socks but for so many hours in the unheated buggy, their feet were numb with cold.

Henry had thought he would only rest but did fall soundly asleep as soon as his body warmed. Hours later, from the looks of the dimming sunlight he awoke to the incessant purring of a large tom cat at his shoulder. Petting the animal, he was immediately given a face wash with a stickery tongue and even louder purring.

"Oh, Good Heavens! You friendly Cat you, get down from there! Oh, Dear, Mr. Thomas, I am so sorry. He really likes people so much and must have pushed your door open. I apologize!"

"No need, he is quite a nice fellow isn't he? I should be up. I had no intention of sleeping so long. Is Timothy Johnson up?"

"He is just washing his hands and face now. I have a nice meal for you. I realize you want to head to the hospitals right away, but please eat a bite first. There will be no food available for you during your search. They are having trouble enough feeding the injured sufficiently to keep them alive, there will be no extra for a visitor."

"Thank you for your kindness and hospitality. It is a privilege to be so well treated! I hope to find my son but realize it may be a lost cause. But I will be hopeful until I have exhausted a thorough search."

"Well, I too hope you find him. It is quite possible you will. Things are very confusing and so many hurt, uniforms of various styles and bodies in various conditions. Not all are conscious, so look carefully. Do not hesitate to move covers and try to see around bandages. I pray you will find the boy you seek. I'll dish the food for you both. Come down as soon as you can."

Henry was angry with himself for not coming sooner. He should have been here right away! What if he had waited too long? Well, no need to hate himself, just get on with it. They both ate the delicious meal provided by Mrs. Hubbard and leaving considerable silver in payment (she certainly wouldn't want confederate money!). They headed out with a jug of hot tea and a large napkin filled with several sandwiches the good woman also provided.

Timothy was talking with a young man of worried expression, dressed in a Union jacket and wool pants. "I would start, Sir, with the two tents to the west of this road. Those are mostly injured Rebels from the area you tell me you have come. And if that doesn't find him, then you will need to take your buggy or other transport and go on the muddy road that heads east. It will take you a couple hours because of the conditions and ruts but you will find three barns along that road. All are unheated but considerable number of Rebels are housed in those, some on cots, some on blankets and some just on straw. A few are lucky enough to have straw ticks made by the Amish. It will take you two days to look over those I believe.

There are so very many and most are not able to speak or fend for themselves."

They did as instructed and looked for several hours among the poor souls in the western area tents. None looked familiar nor were from the same outfit as they needed. The conditions were deplorable! How they survived at all was amazing. Henry became more and more depressed and worried. They must have looked at a thousand or more. All in such bad shape they could not possibly walk home and of course no horses were available – the few fortunate enough to have them would have found the horses confiscated by the Yankees.

By late evening they had lit the candles in their lanterns and were driving the Johnson horses to the east in the general direction they had been instructed to try by the young Yankee soldier that afternoon. The only explanation for the trip was "deplorable"! Ruts, mud, ruined crops, burials, and nothing left that could be described as an actual "road".

Chapter Three

It was late in the middle of their second night by the time they got to the first set of the barns holding innumerable injured soldiers, most but not all, with the uniforms of various Southern troops. Not much rhyme or reason was shown by how they were placed, neither by name nor military outfit. It was just a "look and see" as best they could. Many begged for a ride home and some were so very ill they didn't speak at all. Henry knew he would have nightmares about this trip, no matter how many more years he lived and constantly admonishing himself on being tardy in getting here. Many of the injured had information on where they were from and knew their names, but some were too unfortunately ill to speak or even seem to know what they sought. One thing they were certain of – they had not missed seeing him – they had both looked most closely at each soldier before moving along, often lifting bandages, holding a lantern close and checking hands and body sizes.

It took them over three hours to search each bed in this barn - Henry on the left and Timothy checking the right. They had wonderful help from an Amish man who had taken the description of James Thomas and was assisting them in looking for a blond boy who may be Henry's son. A couple times he would wave them over to such a boy, but unfortunately never finding James. Luckily, Timothy had brought a charcoal stylus and paper and they wrote down a couple names and the hometowns of boys from their general area. They did not promise them a ride home for there was definitely not enough room in the buggy, although large, to take them, but assured they would indeed let their families know. The only good thing was that many were alive and from the general area of north-western Virginia so maybe Henry hoped his Jamie would be found.

It was dawn by the time the exhausted trio had finished the huge barn – times larger than any such barns in their home area. The very helpful Amish gentleman had stayed with them the whole time and said if others came he would remember a lot of the ones looking to return to certain areas in Virginia. They thanked him profusely and getting directions to the next barn, headed out as the sun rose high to find the next temporary hospital and start another search.

When they eventually got to it, anyone's guess was who was the most tired, either of the men or either of the horses. They had stopped at a creek for the animals to drink and given them the rest of the bag of grain Timothy had brought along for them. He hoped he could buy more grain for the trip home from an Amish farm sometime in the coming day or so. This was turning into an expedition of the worst order but they must continue – they had two barns to go!

As they approached the next barn, it was still full daylight outside but with the hint of haze on the horizon. They unhooked two of the lanterns and each took one to use as they looked over the dozens and dozens of injured soldiers in the dark unlit building. It was far more than either of them had imagined in their worst nightmares! A different Army Sargent was their escort and very comforting and helpful. No hint of animosity or opposition as during the war. They couldn't help but feel sorry for the young lad with such distress everywhere. As they proceeded past innumerable beds, being very careful to view each patient and even having to turn a head or uncover a face. None looked familiar. Henry was getting very discouraged but realized they had many soldiers to see yet.

All of a sudden Timothy let out a blasphemy and said: "Howard is that you?" A groan came from the bed and then a cough.

"Mr. Johnson, Sir, are you really here? I did not think I would ever see anyone I knew again." He coughed with considerably obvious pain. "Why are you here, Sir?"

"I am with Henry Thomas. We are seeking Jamie. Have you seen him?"

"Yes, Sir, he is in here somewhere I believe, unless he has died while I slept. He was better yesterday I could hear him talking to the nurse. He was telling her about Charlotte, Sir." About that time their escort came forward and said he knew which soldier this Howard had spoken to, if they would like him to take them?"

"Yes, if you please. We will take both of these boys with us if you will allow Sargent."

"I will not prevent the removal of any of these, they have been declared unfit for service and can return home, if transportation is available. I will take you to the other young man this fellow has spoken to and see if it is the person you seek."

Howard said: "Oh, Sir, you will take me too?"

"Yes, we will. I brought the large carriage, it may not be as comfortable as lying here, but it will indeed get you home, Son!"

Henry had followed the young Army man to the far side of the floor they had just started viewing. He wasn't closer than eight beds or so when a "Yahoo!" was heard and he knew then – he knew that Jamie was alive and well enough to let out the holler he had used when breaking a horse or discovering something else wonderful on the farm!

"Oh, my word, how wonderful to find you! We have looked but not quickly enough. I am so very sorry, Son. I had notification that you were dead but I couldn't accept it nor could Charlotte. So here I am and her father too! We will be taking Howard England back too!"

"I love you Father and prayed you would come. I had no writing instruments to let you know – although one of the Amish men had said they were trying to procure some. They use slates usually but thought their minister could get what I needed. Oh, I cannot tell you how happy I am to see you. I know this is all I need to make me well again. I am still bleeding a good bit from a bayonet stick in the side and my ankle is broken, but I used strips of cloth to bind it tightly and it seems better. Oh thank you for coming, Father!"

Shortly thereafter, with the help of two of the military guards, they had both boys ensconced in the buggy and letting the horses drink from a trough, set out for the long return trip.

"Timothy, we will stop by the nice Mrs. Hubbard's for food and so forth. But we can take turns driving the team and get these fellows back as soon as the horses can. We will stop after Mrs. Hubbard's only for the team to eat and drink or the boys or us to relieve ourselves. But hopefully we can make it in a day and a half."

"That is optimistic but we will try. Even if two or even three days, at least we got what we came for!"

"We did indeed. God Bless, we did indeed!"

Mrs. Hubbard true to her style had provided many things to eat for them to take along and a large bucket of clean water to refill their metal cups. She wished them God Speed and unbeknownst to them a prayer for their safe trip home. Minutes turned into hours and hours into days. Not much talking ensued, both being exhausted and not wanting to wake the two young men, who were so hurt and in constant pain when conscious. They gave them drinks, managed by both holding the youngsters to let them do personal matters beside the road, and trying to make them as comfortable as possible.

They were careful in the dark or even daylight to not make a wrong turn and to avoid the problems with ruts, and swampy areas, and with the river. Also, the difficulty they had coming upon in the Frederick, Maryland area, which was a mass of carriages, wagons, injured soldiers of every description on foot and a few lucky ones on horseback.

It wasn't a parade but it certainly was a conglomeration of human misery!

Leaving Frederick, the road was a little better – taking the mountain gap and trying to negotiate the wagon into the hill country. It took very skillful driving and Henry was particularly thankful for the very strong work horses that Timothy was managing to control. The last two times Jamie had taken something to eat or drink they could not awaken Howard but he was alive and not breathing too badly. Dear Lord, please help these two unfortunate young men!

Suddenly the wagon took a huge uncomfortable bounce and Henry heard Timothy cuss….very unlike him. Please God don't let them have broken a wheel or axel! Both men got down and thankfully nothing appeared broken but the side of the road had been under-washed by rain and the wheel was in a rut up to the hub! They would have to get the boys out of the wagon to lighten the load, even with both men trying to lift it, they couldn't do so because of the weight. Jamie managed to get out with just a little help because of his ankle. Howard was a bigger problem. He was awake and trying to help but he was so very weak! Finally with one man on each side and even Jamie helping they got him out of the carriage and far enough to the side that if it tipped over he would not be hurt even further.

Just as the two older men were wondering if righting the carriage was a lost cause, a young officer in a Union army suit, came up the road. "Oh, Dear, it looks like you have quite a problem. Here let me help – one of you get on the upper side and pull it toward the road – encouraging the horses only when I say - don't touch the wheel but gab a sturdy part of the actual cart. The other two of us will try to lift it out or push it out of the ditch. You young fellows stay well back so if we lose it, you won't be crushed when it falls – always a possibility!"

"Sir, you were driving the team so they will respond to your command the best, be prepared to give the proper command to forward the movement when I say – but not too quickly we have to be certain this hind wheel will clear the road edge! Sir, you, other fellow, we will push it up but also forward out of the ditch at an angle – road isn't as bad just a couple feet along."

Well tarnation, thought Henry, this boy certainly knew how to control a carriage. Such good sense as he was making and a very large strong fellow he was too! Dear God thank you for sending him and for his being so very kind! To help the enemy…well maybe we aren't the actual enemy but the boys are obviously in their gray uniforms.

With every ounce of energy and strength the two very tired men could muster they followed the sensible instructions of the young officer and on the second attempt the carriage gave a great jolt and was again on the road surface. The horses snorting and prancing their feet. Henry had to be careful he didn't fall backward has the wheels jumped the edge of the road, but all was well. The horses were snorting some more, sort of a congratulatory noise, and the men were profuse in their thanks to the rescuer!

"God speed, gentlemen. I am very glad I could help. I have driven carriages before this war and it was fortunate I was here to assist you. Best wishes on the rest of your trip."

Timothy Johnson offered to pay the boy but he was adamant in his refusal. "Not on your life, Sir! It was my pleasure to help…about time I did something God would approve of!" And he rode off in the same direction they were headed.

Henry thought: "Oh, my, we never even got his name to write a note later. Well, as he said, he was doing a good deed for sure and certain." He turned and helped the two young men back into the carriage, while Timothy gave the horses another drink. Howard seemed a little better but too weak to get into the buggy without considerable help. Jamie made it in but he too had difficulty. It would take a good bit of nursing for these fellows to be all right – but it was apparent they would make it. Henry gave them each a drink and then climbed in next to Timothy. "Well, my man, homeward, please!" Timothy laughed.

Hours upon hours later they were beginning to be in familiar territory, passing known farms and the turn off to the country store. By the third nightfall of the trip, they pulled into the lane at the Johnson farm.

Lights were on in most of the windows and just seconds after they were driving in the lane, Charlotte could be seen running toward them at top speed, stumbling in the dark even with her lantern but running as fast as her legs would come. They halted for just a moment for her to see the boys and then continued on through the gate which had been thrown open by staff.

Chapter Four

Homecoming had never been so wonderful! It was a grueling journey and they were telling Charlotte and her mother of their trip. They related that while Jamie managed to suffer through the movement of the carriage and the long journey, Howard was much weaker and would sleep so deeply – or possibly pass out – that they stopped on occasion to bathe his face in water and give him some soup, now cold of course, provided when they had made their good-bye stop at Mrs. Hubbard's.

As they told of their experiences to Charlotte and her family, Henry said he felt Howard would live, but he was in a most precarious state! So many injuries. His own Jamie didn't complain but did appear white as a ghost and moaned in his sleep. Of course, the movement of the carriage was hard on both patients. The roads were terrible for most of the way – having been torn up worse than normal by the war with cannons, wagons, horses and so forth in abundance creating ruts, gullies, humps, and bare rocks. They praised the strong young Union army officer who had anonymously helped them so much.

However, they related that this being the evening of the fifth day, with totally exhausted drivers who had not gotten any sleep for those days, they were delighted to pull into the driveway of the Johnson house.

What a commotion! Crying and laughing and crying and talking and of course kissing by Charlotte! Helen Johnson was busy getting beds warmed and giving the kitchen staff a lot of instruction on fixing foods the young men could eat and would not upset their stomachs. Eggnog was high on the list with applesauce and various breads, of course gravy too. Heating lots of water to give baths and replace awful bandages and clothes – which were immediately burned. Several strong male servants carried the two injured boys to bedrooms and helped with the undressing and bathing. One black servant, the son of their black overseer and who lived in the brick house at the end of the lane was very helpful because he was so strong he could left either boy by himself. Standing a head taller than any of the others, his muscles stretched the sleeves of his linsey-woolsey shirt. Mark, Charlotte's brother, had ridden straight away to the England farm to let them know Howard was back in Virginia and being tended lovingly by his mother, Helen Johnson. He apologized that he hadn't brought Howard home but the rough trip from well north of Gettysburg had taken a toll on him and Mother, Mrs.

Johnson, had insisted she nurse him a couple days before anyone tried to move him again. However, Mrs. England was welcome to come there to see him. Of course, before he finished his sentence she was grabbing a shawl and climbing into the two-seater cart Mark had brought – just on the chance she would want to come.

Charlotte was beside herself! She knew she wasn't being lady-like but did she care? Not on your life! Her Jamie was here, her Jamie was here. She had known in her heart he wasn't killed. She didn't have any idea how, but she had known. Her Mother tried her best to tell her it wasn't "seemly" to be in his bedroom – but pshaw! She didn't care what was "seemly" – Jamie was here, right here in her very house! Enough said. She wiped his brow and held his head while he drank tea and lemonade from the few remaining lemons in the icehouse, not having been able to purchase any this year because of blockades. She made him custard and she brought him some of her Mother's dried pea soup with ham. She hovered and tried innumerable things to make him more comfortable. Finally realizing he needed sleep; she brought her crocheting and a book she hadn't finished reading and just sat in the room beside the table with the oil lamp and where she could occasionally look up and see him there – actually in her house! Oh, thank you God! Thank you!

Henry had quietly looked in one last time on his son before returning home to relieve Carl from doing all the chores alone and to actually sleep in his bed again. He grinned at Charlotte and indicated she did not need to get up. He looked at his son and was satisfied he slept well. My he was exhausted, but happily so…how very relieved he was that he had gone! And to see Mrs. England so grateful too. It was a good trip and he was very satisfied the boys looked like they would get better. Much nursing would be required but they had the spirit to try and that was the biggest advantage. Doctor Weems had come just before Henry left and after examination of both soldiers, had tut tutted but said he didn't see any reason they would not live and have a good life but it would take a lot of nursing, good nutritious food, and they must not be allowed to do too much once they felt well enough to try. Whoever was nursing must watch carefully for any discolored skin, with a greenish tint being alarming and to send for him immediately! Easy does it after so much illness – please see they were not too active. Refusing payment, saying it was his privilege to help, he had left with instructions if either of the soldiers seemed worse like more fever, ride for him immediately.

Henry, not for the first time, thanked Timothy for the trip and complimented him on his marvelous team of horses and fine carriage. He replied it paid for itself many times over by this trip for sure and certain and he would forever be thankful how well it was built and that the wreck beside the road hadn't damaged it too much.

Henry tried to stay alert enough to get his small buggy and horse back to his home and properly unhitched and stabled. The most humorous part of the returning for Henry was watching old Hunter. The dog was ecstatic! He barked; he pressed his head to be pet; he smelled everything Henry had worn, including his boots. He barked some more and finally, after some encouragement he went to his dog dish and ate. It was obvious he had not eaten at all the long time Henry had been gone. Carl reported all was well, the milk in the cold cellar and the most recent in the ice box, the animals fed – except Hunter who wouldn't eat – and everything looked just fine. Oh, also, Doris Rogers had come by to inquire and he had told her about the expedition to Gettysburg. She said to let her know the outcome when he could.

"Carl are you going to town for mail and so forth later today, like you sometimes do?"

"Yes, Henry, I will be going in later this morning now that you are back. I pick up

Master Johnson's mail and drop theirs by the store for them. Would you like me to stop at Ms. Rogers?"

"If you wouldn't mind. It should not be out of your way. Just let her know we brought back Jamie and also the England boy, Howard. Both are quite ill but according to Doctor Weems, should get well with proper care and food, which of course will be done. Helen and Charlotte Johnson was doing all sorts of nice things when I left there."

"I imagine they were! I was hurt during reaping four years ago while helping Timothy and they gave me such good care. I will stop and tell Doris you are back and the successful outcome. I imagine she will call on you shortly thereafter."

"Well don't encourage too soon a visit, I think I could sleep three days running. My I am tired! But how wonderful to see Jamie. He is getting care from Charlotte as well as her mother I would imagine. We can expect a wedding when he is on his feet again."

"Now that's one I would attend! I don't do weddings as a rule, but I would love to see those two married. He would have good help here. She has been raised very comfortably but knows how to work. Quite a good woman – not really a girl anymore. I can still picture her up those trees picking apples with the men – made us all laugh until we realized she was picking more than most of us!" Laughing some more he headed out to get his horse.

The next week was spent resting, visiting Jamie at the Johnson's and doing a lot of gardening, Carl not being inclined to do much but pull some weeds or pick anything getting very ripe. When he was pretty exhausted on about the fifth day, a buggy came up the drive and there was Doris Rogers. He had expected as much. She would want all the details about the hunt for Jamie and so forth. He hoped she had brought lunch because in the evenings he had been too exhausted to fix much and was getting tired of meat and bread (now called sandwiches after some English Earl he thought) and canned peaches or pears.   Well, goodness, he reckoned she <u>had</u> brought something. Taking a huge picnic basket out of her buggy, he went quickly to help her – it was half as big as she – of course that still wasn't huge – Doris weighing less than a hundred pounds soaking wet!

"What in the world have your brought, my Dear? This is very heavy. I can smell fried chicken I bet. How grand that will taste."

"You men are all the same. The smell of fried chicken is always a favorite. I did indeed fry two chickens – just leaving a few pieces for Mable. And a blueberry pie, of course, I haven't known you for years to not learn of your penchant for blueberry pie, Henry!"

"Well, here is that fine dog. No! No! You are not to eat that chicken, my fine brown fellow! Oh, dear, Henry, he really is interested in that. Maybe you better carry the basket of chicken and I will tote the other things."

"Down! Hunter! Down! I have never seen him so impolite, however he didn't eat the whole time I was gone to Pennsylvania so he is probably trying to make up for it. We'll be careful to put the chicken in the center of the table where he cannot reach or we will have a greasy mess on the floor and no luncheon! I'm afraid his manners are not the best."

"Well, I doubt I would be as messy but if I went without eating for several days, I may be just as interested in a platter of chicken."

Henry was laughing so hard he could hardly open the door and still maintain his hold on the lunch items. He realized that Doris made him laugh just as Carole Ann had. Henry offered to do his green beans again and she said they were definitely a favorite of hers so he started browning some cuttings of country ham while he went to the pantry for two jars of green beans. He would need to can those again this year too. He ate a good many of them and evidently Doris liked them too. She had little room for a garden in her city back yard, just tomatoes, lettuce and onions or so. He would plan to share what he put up.

Adding the green beans to the browning ham scraps, he also added a little of the tan sugar and soon they had a good meal with some bread she had baked and brought in the other big basket. He had a skillet of potatoes she had peeled and sliced for him while he had done the other things.

What a feast! Chicken, green beans, fried potatoes, fresh bread and blueberry pie! He was afraid he had not been very polite but my he was so hungry for good food! The meal at Mrs. Hubbard's seemed weeks ago.

"Doris, how can I ever thank you! You are such an excellent cook and I had gone without several meals in my quest for Jamie. Thank you so much! You are very thoughtful. I hope to see you at church Sunday. I know I don't attend often enough but I really need to properly thank God for the return of Jamie! I will prepare a country ham and if you and your sister would like, you may join me after church. I will do a caramel flan too." And he grinned knowing he had hit the nail on the head with caramel.

"You drive a hard bargain. We will be glad to join you! Would you mind awfully if I very impolitely ask if Mable may bring Tom Weston too? He is joining us for church and it would be so nice for him to get to know you. He moved in next to us three years ago. He has never been married – his sweetheart having been killed by a run-away horse. I think he is sweet on Mable, if you want my opinion."

"That would be just fine. I have heard nice things about the gentleman from Mr. Johnson of the newspaper with his office beside the railroad station but not had the pleasure of his company. We will make dinner for four then. And thank you so much for today. Delicious, as always just really delicious!"

"Thank you for including him, I'm certain Mable will be pleased."

He watched her carriage go out the road and thought again how nice she is and how lonely it was here without his dear wife. How would she have felt about him taking another bride? Well, she would be all right with it, he felt certain. They hadn't talked a lot about such things, but when she was so very ill, she had told him to find a companion. It was no honor to her to be lonely. As much as that hurt at the time, he saw now she was correct…he would see how things went along but Doris was a lovely person...just maybe it would be nice to be married again.

He cleaned up his kitchen mess, having not let Doris help with needing to accomplish her hour ride back home. As he mused on her being here, he also wondered how that would fit in with Jamie and Charlotte. Well, probably all right. They would most likely build their own home on the hill to the east of the main house, eventually. He, of course, wouldn't require it – this house was big enough but it would give them privacy and maybe with luck they would fill it with children. Grandchildren – now there was a pleasant idea to fall asleep on!

While it didn't take him long to go to sleep, he did think on the many changes to take place shortly…weddings. He had thought of weddings – plural! Well, how about that now, so his mind was already including Doris in the family plans. Not too bad an idea at all. He would miss his dear wife forever, but his heart could hold another. And he knew Doris got along well with both Charlotte and Jamie, It would be a happy home for them all. And the woman could cook! She would fit into the busy life they would have with all the improvements he planned.

As he drifted off, finally, he was smiling – not very usual for him lately but smiling he was!

He dreamt of his son and his dead wife. He dreamt of his farm and expanding it with his son having an interest in the crops and animals. He dreamt of the great life he had enjoyed for so many years with a loving spouse and an intelligent and very hard-working son. Then his dreams turned into a nightmare where he was searching for Jamie and couldn't find him among the victims of the war.

Finally, he woke to the dawn and realized his son was indeed healing and he didn't have any reason for nightmares. Well, so much for bad memories!

Chapter Five

The week sped by and he was so very busy. Things were needing a lot of attention on the farm and he had hired Tommy Place to come and help him. The boy was not very experienced with farm work, living in town with his parents, but was a very willing worker and seemed to understand instruction. He had his own horse and handled it well – a big advantage in not having to train him to ride. He wasn't afraid of the other animals either, like some boys Henry had tried to use. He mentioned a reasonable price for working a whole day and Tommy agreed. Henry was hoping it wasn't a waste of money at the time. However, it proved to be very advantageous. The boy was willing, smart, strong and limber. By his second try he could attach the plow, put on the work saddle and strap up the horse. Much quicker than others Henry had shown. He had a good commanding voice and the horse, although looking back at him in the beginning, was soon realizing the boy was in charge and following instructions in "horse talk" such as "Gee", "Haw", and "Halt".

By the second evening Henry realized he didn't have to follow behind the lad and check how things were put away. They were not only in the proper place but cleaned off from remaining plant parts or soil. Tommy even knew how to clean the hooves of the faithful horse. He asked if Tommy would like to ride to the Smyth property to look at some young horses, and he was agreeable, in fact excited to do so.

The next morning, they headed in the Smyth direction and it wasn't long with both riding instead of in a carriage, that they arrived in the lane.

A dark servant came immediately and took both their mounts. Henry thanked him and the two headed to the house where Tom stood on the porch to greet them.

"Hey, Tom, I would like you to meet my new worker – this is Tommy Place. You should have no trouble remembering his name." As everyone laughed Tom extended a hand to the young man and they shook. "I have come to look over those young colts you have. I thought about them all the while I was on the trip to Gettysburg. I guess you heard we brought my Jamie back and Howard England too. Both are still ill but should get better according to Dr. Weems."

"I did indeed hear – how fortuitous that you knew to go. I thought you had gotten word he died there?"

"I did indeed get an "official notification" but evidently from what I heard in Gettysburg and rumored here – such notices are not to be relied upon. Thank the Good Lord Above! I am afraid young Howard has a long road ahead but he is young and strong – with the very best of care by Helen Johnson."

"Oh, goodness, she is a marvel. Efficient, knowledgeable and caring. She nursed my Ethel when she was so very ill two years ago and Doctor Weems felt she may not get well. But she did and it is greatly in thanks to Helen! You two come in and we will talk about the horses over some tea and tell me what you want them for. I have eight in total

– you probably have only seen the two I intend to keep that are usually along the fence near the road – but I have six others to show you. One in particular seems to take to a pulling-collar quite well."

"With Jamie home and probably a wedding in the near future, I think we will expand the farm. I had wanted to and then my darling Carole Ann got sick, then the war took Jamie, so I haven't taken up Reynolds offer to buy the three very large fields of his that adjoin mine. I can do so now and his price is quite reasonable – so therefore I am looking for horses!"

"Tommy will you be interested in continuing to work for me, do you think?"

"Oh, I would love to! I have always wanted to farm but of course we have no land and father is with the railroad so not really interested, but I would love to farm. You set a good example, Sir, so I hope to work for you quite a while."

Henry had the time of his life that afternoon. He pet horses, fed horses and talked to horses.

He found a young mare that he really liked and Tom assured him there was an unrelated stallion that he may like as well if he was interested in breeding the mare. Henry said he would talk it over with

Jamie but buying the extra-large fields, he may indeed like to do so. They talked the price of horses, with young Tommy taking it all in, amazed at the discussion and the prices being mentioned. The boy had no idea horses were so expensive!

Henry picked the two recommended by Tom but said he would be wishing Jamie to see them too, as soon as he was able. Tom agreed Jamie should see them and suggested he would keep them but not sell to anyone else, until Jamie could make up his mind. On that fine note Henry and Tommy left and headed to the Johnson's to see how the two boys were doing. They were already two-thirds of the way there, so may as well.

Imagine how surprised Henry was when he and Tommy road up, to see none other than Jamie sitting on the front porch with Charlotte knitting beside him. He was reading a book and looked up surprised when he heard the hoofbeats. What a reunion! Much hugging (and crying by Charlotte) ensued. He was hobbling considerably with his broken foot not completely healed but he assured he was just feeling very well!

Henry was elated and Charlotte said that Doctor Weems would be by in three days and probably release him to go home – providing he was very careful with the foot and with his rib bandage. She said she would rebandage the foot properly for him and put a "walking board" in the bandage as recommended by the doctor. It would substitute as a shoe but not protect the foot real well so caution would be needed.

Hearing the commotion on the porch both Timothy and Helen came out. Nothing would do but the visitors stay to dinner and Tommy seemed quite out of his element but at least kept his manners enough to thank them. The meal was delicious and Henry helped carry the evening meal up to Howard, who was much improved but still stayed mostly in his bed on the doctor's orders. His mother came a couple days at a time and Mr. Johnson had promised to carry him home in the luxurious big carriage by the end of the week. Dr. Weems had given many instructions and felt his mother would take good care.

By the time Henry and Tommy got back home, it was getting quite dark and they had to tend the animals with lanterns lit and were careful where they walked and set the lanterns down. With the two of them, it didn't take very long to tend to the various stalls, including throwing some more feed to the pigs and chickens, although the chickens were at roost for the night. At least Henry knew he wouldn't have to cook any supper but would offer the boy a piece of cake before bedtime. He didn't realize how lonely he had become, even with Hunter around – as faithful as the old dog was, it was nice having another person in the house. Just made him think once again about Doris and if possibly she would be interested in marrying such an old fuddy duddy, as he!

Chapter Six

The few days that Jamie remained at the Johnson house, Henry had rewashed his bedding and cleaned the room nicely. He was so very anxious to see his son properly home once again.

Just a few days later, Jamie was actually here! He was in the house and ensconced in his old bedroom. How wonderful was that. The move had left him too tired to eat the many things his father had prepared in celebration of the home coming but that was all right...it had helped Henry pass the time. As prearranged, Timothy Johnson had driven him in the large comfortable carriage with Charlotte hovering to take care of his every need. It was a combination of amusing and emotional. The poor girl had indeed loved him for a long time and still did. Using Timothy, Henry and Tommy they got him upstairs to his old room.

Charlotte followed along behind with a bed warmer, full of hot coals from the range and wrapped in towels to keep it from being too hot on his legs. She had prepared a tray of scones, a pitcher of hot tea, and ham biscuits, which Tommy rushed down to retrieve. She had sweetened the tea just as he liked and he chuckled at all the attention.

Eating a little of everything to please them all, he finally admitted he was tired from all the day's activity and would like to sleep. Kissing him without apology, Charlotte led the way downstairs after his father had removed the tray and covered him lovingly with the quilt his mother had made for him many years ago. HE WAS HOME! The last thought he had before drifting into a sound sleep.

Henry said goodbye to the guests thanking them profusely for all the care and attention to Jamie and said good night to Tommy as he went upstairs in the other end of the house to what had become his room. Henry did not go back to his own bedroom, however. He and Hunter instead went into Jamie's room and Henry prepared to sleep in the large rocker with a small coverlet over him. After carefully sniffing the returned boy in the bed, Hunter laid down beside it on the rug and sighed. As he put his feet up on the stool, Henry drifted off to sleep after chuckling at the dog expressing the same feelings he had – the lost was home!

The next morning Henry was chagrined when he discovered Jamie had been up and used the slop jar and taken a drink of tepid tea without waking his father. However, Hunter had not missed a thing and was devouring a day-old biscuit on the rug by the bed.

Looking up sleepily, Henry asked what Jamie wanted for breakfast and he immediately said hot cakes and ham, please. Hunter woofed that the same would be good for him and a very happy father went downstairs to prepare it. Luckily Tommy had already laid a fire and brought in the eggs saying he was on his way out to milk and would eat later.

Henry fixed the requested hot cakes and ham – also scrambling some eggs, frying some bacon and heating the maple syrup as he remembered his son preferred. He made a pitcher of tea, knowing Jamie had never liked coffee much.

Jamie made it down the stairs without difficulty using a cane with a forked bottom to ascertain steadiness, made by the overseer at Charlotte's home. As they ate together for the first time in months, Henry felt blessed. Suddenly Jamie wanted to know how soon his father thought a wedding could be held.

Laughing, Henry said they probably should talk to the minister so bans could be read, but after that, just as soon as they wanted. Didn't Charlotte need time to make a dress or such?

"Oh, no, Father, she already made her dress and has her closet all rearranged with the things she wants to bring here separated. All Hazel, her maid would need to do is pack them or layer them in a carriage for the short trip here.

I asked her repeatedly if she was certain she wanted to keep to her promise, now that I am hurt but she was furious with me and said of course she would marry me unless I had changed my mind...well, as you know, I would NEVER do so. Perfect women don't come along every day. And she is certainly perfect!" Whereupon he took his fourth hot cake and another full slice of salted ham.

Henry went out on the porch to laugh. He noticed that Hunter did not come out with him. Although Jamie was still eating that may have been the enticement but Henry had to be quite stern with the dog to get him to leave Jamie even to take care of "business", it was like the dog was afraid Jamie would leave again....well, don't let anyone tell you dogs aren't smart!

Shortly after breakfast, Hunter set to his barking that notified them someone was about but it was his "friendly" bark with no anger so they knew it was a person familiar to them. Sure, and certain, there was Charlotte and her parents. They came with a basket covered in a cloth and Henry imagined it was some treat or other for Jamie.

"I am so very sorry to bother you Papa Henry, but I had to see Jamie. How is he? Can I see him please?"

Before Henry could answer, Jamie spoke from the porch door. "Oh, you may see me anytime you wish, Dear Heart. I am up and about and just ate the most wonderful breakfast! Can we fix something for you?"

"Oh, goodness me, we are such a bother!" exclaimed Helen Johnson.

"You are never a bother!" responded Henry. Come on in. Our boy is indeed very fine. He made it downstairs under his own strength and has eaten me almost out of house and home for his breakfast! Notice how Hunter won't leave his side and the dog guarded him all night beside the bed! We are all very happy to have him here, but I realize you want to see him too, Dear. Come on in here – all of you! Can I fix some more breakfast? I have many eggs and country ham and can whip up more batter for cakes, too!"

"No, we have eaten but thank you. Charlotte barely let us finish eating at home until we had to come in the carriage to see how Jamie was doing."

Helen unveiled a basket and it contained blueberry preserves – Jamie's favorite and also some canned peaches, knowing Henry had said he was getting low. "I put up way too many peaches last year for our crop was abundant and I couldn't let them go to waste. We gave some to various families and I even canned some for the bachelors or ill. Please share these."

Jamie grinned. "I will have a jar with luncheon. Thank you! I should be ready to eat again in an hour or so, I believe."

"What? You just got up from the table after eating four hot cakes the size of the stove burner and untold ham! Even some of "my" eggs having said you didn't want any when I was cooking!"

While everyone laughed, Jamie didn't try to apologize. "I hope you have come to discuss the wedding. I am feeling so much the better. I should be able to help with light tasks within the week, as long as my side doesn't reopen. My ankle is much improved!"

"How wonderful!" exclaimed Charlotte. "Yes, I had hoped you still wanted to get married soon, as you had said while still at our house! Do you indeed, want to do so?"

"I'm afraid I can't right now, my jacket needs brushing and my hair trimmed but maybe tomorrow?" said Jamie laughing.

"Oh, my goodness! Aren't you the pair! Well, I can get a lot done for Charlotte in short order, since her dress is ready. The minister has talked to us and I assume you as well to be certain he should still plan such a thing. We will be honored to host the reception – after the light refreshment at the church we thought a full meal at our house might be nice. Is that satisfactory with both of you, Charlotte and Jamie?"

"Well, it is with me! Darling what do you think?" Inquired Jamie.

"Whatever suits the parents, is fine with me. I personally do not need so much attention. Just a sweet ceremony and you beside me forever is all I can ask. Henry, I don't want to put you out, but we can use Jamie's bedroom as our own – there is not a need for a "bridal suite" as is talked about in the cities. What can we help with or what else needs to be done? My maid is quite ready to help with clothes or anything and I would wish no trip or such celebration….just a wedding in church is my only requirement!" Said Charlotte.

"Oh, daughter, you are so forward! Perhaps the boy is not ready to undertake such an adventure! He is just home and still not completely well. Aren't you hurrying things too much?" Asked Timothy Johnson.

"Oh, Sir, please do not scold her! We had talked at length while you so kindly provided me rest but we both are quite ready to be married! I plan on taking part in the farm here immediately. I know I cannot fully do the work of a good man, yet...but I will. I am better each day! And now Father has purchased the extra fields, we have a lot to do with Tommy's help. I can supervise from a wagon until completely healed and I know Charlotte can take part and be of interest."

"Oh, you know me so well, Darling. I will be most happy to take an interest in getting the new fields ready and in the fall fruit picking and so forth. I love climbing trees! We will order more jars and wax for canning season, and I am perfectly capable of assisting with that, as Mother can tell you!"

Henry was laughing so hard he had to sit down. "Timothy, come over here and take a

chair. I think we have a wedding all planned and the canning season as well – all we old folks need to do is stand back and watch!" and he continued laughing.

Everyone could tell that Helen was a bit put out at her daughter and future son-in-law but she ended up smiling as she too took a seat. And when asked, made many suggestions about the ceremony and moving things like clothes and some furniture from her home to the Thomas house. About that time, Tommy came in from his morning chores. He immediately started to back out of the room.

"Wait, Tommy, don't go! I need to know if you will stand up for me with father. I am getting married!"

"I would be so very honored! I do have a Sunday jacket, but not much else in the way of clothes – I would not want to embarrass you on such an important day."

Timothy spoke up and said he believed they were close enough in size to use a pair of his trousers and that left Charlotte to check with her bridesmaid.

She spoke immediately and said Judith Patton was all prepared and even had her dress made. They had been corresponding and met the previous week to finalize all they needed to do. When that name – Judith Patton – was mentioned it was noted by most that

Tommy Place was blushing furiously….well what do you know, evidently he knew Judith Patton!

And so, following a discussion that very afternoon with the minister, it was determined that James Halsted Thomas would be the happy groom for Charlotte Elizabeth Johnson the following Saturday a week in their little country church with a reception in the manse and then a complete dinner at Wildwood, Charlotte's home – with all the members of the church invited.

Henry just sat down and shook his head. Things would be on the "go" around here from now on he was sure and certain. For the way this couple could get things done, life would be interesting. He wouldn't doubt the new fields would be in production by next year with such organization.

My goodness! Doris Johnson would need to be informed and he should tell Jamie about his plans that included her. He and Hunter would have to learn to get out of the way…times were changing at the Thomas house!

THE END

Author's note: With the difficulty of being at war for four years, things were not always so quickly arranged by most families. But others had been anxious to follow their desires and waited with baited breath. So many had the pain of funerals and others the happier weddings to be planned. Everyone had been relieved to get things as close to normal as could be done after such devastation.

The following years would be hard for many in the south. Not as bad in Virginia as some southern states – such as Georgia and Alabama where things were burned, no workers available and crops died…but a great effort was made by all Southerners to overcome the devastation and find relief and happiness where they could.. As many years would tell, the

South did "rise again" and happiness would be found, but sad memories prevailed.

Book Two – The Bravery at VMI

Chapter One

Master Sergeant William Johnson was observing his "troops". Such a sad sight as he had never seen before! They were all in accord, standing straight at attention, Virginia Military Institute (VMI) uniforms properly suited, and eyes straight ahead. Had they been men, they would have been a perfect unit...but unfortunately none were men. Boys, just boys. This sad lot were the youngest. Many of the older cadets had been dispatched to areas of fighting already and were in actual Confederate army units. Here some were as young as fifteen and he had found at least two who had changed their papers and were thirteen and fourteen but the Commandant had no way to send them home without them probably being killed anyway, so they may as well fight! They did each have a proper rifle and seemed to know what to do with it. He wasn't a praying man as a rule, feeling discipline and training took care of things.   But Dear God, please protect this unit. Please!

The VMI Corp and General Breckenridge's confederate forces near Staunton had marched eighty-five miles Northward to New Market, Virginia and arrived five days later on May 15, 1864. Union troops under General Franz Sigel were atop Bushong's Hill using cannon and musketry.   Breckenridge had been ordered by Army Major Charles Semple to send in the Corp but he refused. With almost all of these only fifteen years old (the older cadets elsewhere but nearby) and at a great geographic and terrain disadvantage, they would be slaughtered. Other cadets did however, close the gaps in Confederate forces while they regrouped and greatly helped push the Union Army back. Breckenridge did then successfully force Sigel back in a form of retreat. It was a bloody, close fight.

Many of the Cadets were barefoot because the plowed ground was muddy and it sucked the boots right off the boys. Those same boys were doing "clean-up" -

finding and recovering implements of war as were available and burying the dead.

All cadets were then ordered to march to Richmond where they were awarded for bravery by Southern President Jefferson Davis and Virginia Governor William Smith. However, when arriving after another long and difficult march they eventually had to "step out" a third time, all the way back at their post at VMI in Lexington. Much to their regret, finding Union General David Hunter had attacked it and ordered it burned – the date had been March twelfth eighteen sixty-four. Right after they had left for New Market.

Putting out fires and using as much of the solid walls as possible, the young force regrouped and in October 1864 again marched forth and were dispatched to Richmond to be assigned trench duty. They were, of course, totally exhausted when they arrived at the Poe farm where academic duties resumed at Alms House in December 1864.

After all their bravery and great losses, the Corp remained there until Virginia

Military Institute again reopened as an academic institution on October 17, 1865, which was after the surrender of General Lee to General Grant earlier that year.

Meanwhile, before the armistice, the parents of the students had little information regarding their condition or even where they were. Some scattered reports were issued and what newspapers could be printed would, on occasion, mention the brave young men, including many being killed and injured. Sometimes listing actual students but often not. Injured were usually taken into private homes to recuperate while most of the dead were buried with other military losses. But very little good information was coming to the parents. Most not knowing if their boys lived or died.

In Frederick County – near Winchester, this was the situation for Mildred Adams, who was beside herself! She was never a patient woman anyway, nor overly cordial, although generous to the less fortunate. Well thought of as a strong church member but right now, though, they should see her! She knew she was less than Godly! Nothing would do but Robert would go to VMI. As a mother she had objected but he and his father had ignored her concerns. Certainly, when he left the war had not been declared but she knew – anyone knew that had a brain – that war seemed inevitable. Of course, she was correct. She was always correct! If times were "normal" he would be graduating shortly – but times were far from "normal" and his studies were interrupted with having to fight in the war. They had not heard from him in some months. Dear God, above, where is Robert?

Now that an armistice was signed, some students were again studying but evidently mail had not recuperated as well as one would wish. Finally, Mildred had "had enough" and demanded her husband, Raymond, ride to Lexington and find out what was what with Robert. He replied for her to write, which made her livid. She informed him she HAD written six letters – some to Robert and some to the authorities all without satisfactory responses. He WOULD go as she wished or she would hitch the buggy and go herself. Of course, this wasn't done – but she could easily set a precedent – for her patience was over and it was time to find out all they could about their son! Her husband took one look at her, realized she probably would indeed go south – the results of the recent war not withstanding - and so he put on his coat, requesting Ray, their black man in charge of the stables, to hitch the buggy with two of the best horses.

Finally, she had action from somewhere. Not more than two hours after Raymond had gone, there was a commotion by the dogs and to her surprise Mr. Johnson of the telegraph office was coming up the walk. Her butler was home today with his ailing wife, so she was tending the door. Hushing her three guard dogs and opening the door welcomingly, she asked what had brought him. He handed her a paper to read and there was a listing: first of the known cadets who were killed and then of the ones ascertained to be back at the badly damaged school – or in appropriate housing, such as elsewhere in Lexington or near it until repairs were finished. Robert was on that list! Hallelujah! Both lists were stated to be incomplete and in no way accounted for the whole student body nor any in army hospitals, but at least her son was listed as alive…my how grateful she was! Mr. Johnson wouldn't agree to stay to eat anything but needed to continue on to several other homes, some with good news and some bad. Not too many in the area had boys at VMI but he knew which did and would give them all the report he could. She quickly handed him some cookies and a flagon of tea and thanking him again she went back to the kitchen stove and to assist Mabel with many kitchen duties.

Mildred could just imagine her husband's ire, when he made the long trip and later found out she had gotten information in the wake of his leaving…well, so be it. Who would have guessed after she had tried so valiantly to know something? With his gray hair and proper papers, she assumed her man would not be given any difficulty by any Union troops as to his traveling. He was probably mad enough at her to set any such inquiry straight. She smiled to herself feeling she would be on the receiving end of such ire as the several days passed it would take for his return. Hopefully he would actually see their Robert and be able to tell her, when he was willing to speak to her again, what shape the boy was in and what he had done the past months.

She was correct, as she would not have been surprised to note that things in Lexington were not good. The place was a shambles and every house with a spare room was full. Meals were a problem with some food shortages but the local merchants and farmers were trying their best to accommodate the young men who had been so brave and were exhausted and many injured. Homeowners, wives and staff were put in the position of nurses and care givers and beds or at least mattresses were set up in parlors and even dining rooms.

Chapter Two

The following day, Mildred set about making her cough syrup again. She had two dozen bottles just three months ago but chest coughs were raging in the area and she had attended many who were ill. Even though it was now early summer, the chest problems continued. Poor Mrs. Henry. She prayed the good woman would get well. She had made a poultice for her chest and provided extra salve for the maid to attend her on her last visit to "town". When this batch of syrup was ready, she would make it her first stop this trip. She hoped many would return the empty syrup bottles to her for refilling She had listed six houses who would need some and had let her accompanying servant know they would be out most of the afternoon to deliver it all. Maybe even until dark if she heard of others she didn't know were ill when she started out.

With her frown and determined look, her new maid timidly approached her. There was a man inquiring if she could give him somewhat to eat, must she send him away, he looked quite ill? Seeing the new girl, "Alice" looking confused she said: "Here, Alice, you stir this – mind it does not stick – it has honey and dark sugar in it – it must be stirred all the while or it will burn in the bottom. I'll go see what he wants."

Not being a stupid woman, she called for Joshua, who served as butler, to accompany her to the door. Joshua was one of their free darkies and as trusted as any man. He came willingly and stood behind her, all six and a half feet of him.

The dogs were growling and had their hackles up – standing close behind as well. The beggar looked alarmed at the size of her companion, for he towered over her short stature, and great big dogs too! "What do you need, Sir?" Mildred asked.

"I, I, I am attempting to walk back to my home in North Carolina. I was released from a hospital near Gettysburg six days ago, ago. I caught a couple rides, rides, with Amish, but not enough. I have run out of food, food, and would beg that you might provide me with meat and bread, Miss. If you please Miss." He stuttered.

"Tell me your name and something about yourself and I will not only feed you but see you have a ride and fare for the train at the station in Winchester. Now speak up!"

"Oh, God Bless you, Missy! That would be much more than I had prayed for. I am William Pence Wallace and I am from Charlotte, North Carolina but my folks may have gone to relatives in the Georgia hills to avoid the fighting. I was part of an infantry group that was not supposed to go to Gettysburg – but somehow we marched there anyway. It took too long a trip so we missed most of the war there but many of my fellow men are dead. If I had not been unconscious, I would probably be in a Yankee lockup, but by the time I had my senses back, they had moved on and a nice lady in Frederick, Maryland gave me a flagon of homemade brew and a meat sandwich. She suggested I head south as soon as ever I could and maybe I would not be found and incarcerated. So here I am, I came through the gap and down the Pike past Cross Junction and Gainesboro. My boots are worn through but I put bark and pieces of my shirt tail in the bottoms – not the most comfortable footwear but I made it here!"

Turning her head, she said: "Joshua, go to the eastern spare bedroom and find that old pair of riding boots of the Master and bring them. I think they should fit this fellow he looks about Robert's size and Robert could wear those. Also bring a sandwich – no two sandwiches and a couple apples and a block of cheese, then a flagon of water. Give them to the boy now. There will be other things I will put in a cloth bag – like I use to take the medicines when I visit the ill."

"You, young man, have a seat in the rocker on the porch. My man will bring you some repast to eat now while you rest and a new pair of socks. He will take care of the rest then drive you to the train station." Nodding her head briskly with her normal serious determination. After being certain the boy had taken the chair, she shut and locked the door and went to check on her cough syrup and get the socks and food for the poor soldier. She was a very careful person and locking the door came naturally to her…such terrible goings on the last four or more years. No sense in taking any chances. She was not worried about the fellow trying to take the carriage from Joshua…not if he wanted to live! Joshua weighed him twice and had fought for his freedom when a boy – Joshua could take care of anything! He was a most loyal servant and had a wife and three young children in the house just up the road. A house given to him by her husband after he completed two years training with them and gave the very best service possible. She had insisted he be her butler although he had been prepared to continue working in the fields. She needed protection with the war breaking out back then and was confident that Joshua would give her any help he could. He was sterling and she liked making cookies for his children every so often.

She went to the clothesline on the back porch and took down a dry pair of her husband's socks, found a flagon with cork stopper for tea, and wrapped meat in some bread, putting that in a cloth sack and adding two apples and a pear plus six cookies. She made cookies by the dozens every week – she could spare six for such a boy to take in this bag for traveling.

After seeing Joshua and their visitor off with train money, she continued to make the medicine and bottle it. She retained enough to fill a lidded crock of the same for their use.

Glad to see Joshua had not taken her good carriage, she could start delivering the medicine she had made including taking some of her camphor. Then she filled another basket, putting in some preserves and jellies. She had a full day of it. Taking Big Jim, another one of the black servants with her, she headed out on her errands telling Mary to watch the place and not let the dogs out until she returned nor open the door to anyone she didn't know. It was wonderful the way Raymond had trained the dogs to be so protective. He was very interested in history and had studied how, for centuries, dogs had protected their owners, the small children in the nurseries of kings and any castle property. He further looked into how to train them, finding good information from several foreign countries, like Germany, and Sweden – where dogs protected royalty, children, even animals such as horses of the rich. Although trained to attack in dangerous situations, such dogs would be very loving and friendly to their owners or those the owners loved. Well, Robert certainly had done an excellent job! Their dogs were wonderful and she felt quite safe with their good training at protecting the place and those in it.

As they left, she drove the carriage. When Big Jim drove, she left fingerprints in the upholstery. But he would be handy for running things into the various houses and also protection, just in the event they ran into anyone intent on doing them harm. She noticed he had a pistol, ammunition and a long knife, which was his normal trademark. He had kept the knife since a boy, it being used by his father who had been a mistreated slave. She had never heard the details and was very certain she didn't want to! She was not at all afraid of Big Jim but was aware that he had few black friends and was given a wide berth on occasion. It was unusual for a black to be armed but she was glad he was.

Her husband had always been cautious about Big Jim and usually amazed that she trusted him so much and rode with him to the market at the Springs or on other errands, as she was doing today. However, the boy called her "Missy" and was always polite to her, helping her mount or dismount and carrying her packages. She was never bothered by beggars or other 'ner'do'wells when Big Jim was the driver or when he otherwise accompanied her!

Her first stop was indeed to see Mrs. Mabel Henry and things were not good there. Without a by-your-leave she started giving instruction to the young girl trying to attend to the needs of Mrs. Henry. The girl obviously not doing so with much success. In her forthright manner Mildred instructed the girl to move a bed or cot into the kitchen nearer the stove and place her mistress on it with all the pillows she could find so her mistress was elevated to breathe best. Then boil water continually until her mistress' breathing was better. Every four hours she was to boil an additional small pot with water and four tablespoons of the mixture she was leaving. Make certain her mistress was close to the pot and breathing the steam. With all that, hopefully her mistress would be better in three days. Feed her any broth she would take and any fruit or fruit juice – not to worry too much about meat and vegetables, when a little better maybe some vegetable soup. Should the girl know how, it would be nice if she stewed some chicken parts and gave the broth and some pieces of diced chicken to her mistress as well. If her stomach turned, give her bread without butter – sweet bread would be good if they had it. Making certain the girl understood all the instructions and saying if Mrs. Henry was not better in three days to ride immediately or send someone for the doctor.

Finally, she took care of all her other stops and errands in her usually efficient and quick manner. With Big Jim dutifully assisting as instructed, she got many amazed looks while in town with her very noticeable companion, who was armed which was very unusual for any black man – freed or not. As she made her many stops, she was telling those who thanked her profusely that it was "nothing" and hoped they or their family would soon be well. Mildred did mention Mrs. Henry's condition to Helen Price – a most kind and conscientious woman, also God fearing – knowing she would check on Mrs. Henry as she could.

She never realized she was the "talk of the town" with her odd companion and generous caring for the ill. But it wouldn't have mattered anyway, it was something that needed to be done – so she did it! And her companion was none of their business...but a great aid to her and made her feel much safer than if she traveled alone.

Her husband was not back the next two days and she was very worried he had come upon a problem, but hoped he was just checking on their son and taking his time to travel.

She and staff had put away all the medication and were busy tearing up some muslin for fresh bandages. The garden took a lot of her time that day and the next. Having devoted some time to the poor boy returning home and for her medicine cooking and delivery, she had ignored her garden. Taking two of the regular servant girls with her and with Big Jim in attendance – much to the fright of the two additional part-time girls, with the regulars not giving him a second thought – they worked in the garden for hours on end. However, it was done with good results.

They had filled the baskets in the dry cellar, cooked and canned many other items, and left the garden in pristine condition without a weed in sight. Staff had even "rescued" two quart-cups of berries, enough to have for breakfast for everyone the following morning, and also found some other "out of season" items to pick as well for immediate use. Her favorite were the peas and she was very pleased to see the plants had kept producing well past their normal stage. They had pulled the plants after rescuing the late peas for today's use. Such mild weather was really good for the garden and had meant there was more produce than she would have expected.

That night she tried to sleep; she was certainly tired enough to – but she just couldn't! Where in tarnation was Robert? And a further problem – where was Raymond and why wasn't he home yet? Please Lord, don't let him be shot as a spy or something! It was done and with very little forethought by the shooters. He didn't appear armed, did have a gun hidden in the carriage, but definitely wasn't in uniform. He should be HOME by now!

Several days later, as dawn broke and still "worried to death", she got dressed and headed out to gather eggs and milk the cow. It would astonish her staff but when she was upset, she worked and she had done more of all the medications a day ago, canned for days before that. Then had done the garden and yesterday she had reorganized all her kitchen cabinets, checked the spice and storage "safe", the dining room drawers, cleaned the ice box and put a new pail down to catch the melting ice.

Of course, it was some days before when she had delivered her medicines and helped the North Carolina boy get home. So today, she would bother staff…she had to do something! As she dressed she saw the present for Charlotte Johnson and James Thomas, who would be married soon, she felt, although the boy was quite injured. What a great couple, she hoped they would like her gift. She had ordered a silver tea service from England and with the war ending was not at all certain it would ever come but it had and was now nicely wrapped in some silk cloth with a big silk flower adornment…Things Carolina could use for making underwear and a dresser decoration later.

She had been out quite a while this morning, checking on many crops and plants besides getting the eggs and milking. As she approached the house again, with Big Jim carrying her eggs and milk, she noticed a man on the porch. There are many wanderers or deserters about now the war is almost at an end. It is not safe. "Jim, do me a favor, let me take this food, while you see what the man wants. You will hopefully get an honest answer." She quickly took the items, struggling with the heavy milk jug and they continued to the porch, where Jim started an inquisition of the most serious note!

"I am just looking for something to eat, please. I am trying to make it back to Pennsylvania. I have my papers. I realize you are Confederate sympathizers but would beg you to help me. I have walked a long way." As Big Jim kept a distance between them Mildred requested to look at his papers.

With apparent reluctance, the man handed them over, watching her carefully. She wondered if he thought she would destroy them out of meanness.

"I know the Union Commandant quite well. Would you like to have a ride to the encampment at Gerrardstown?"

"I can do so, Ma'am, but it would put a much longer treck to my home, Missus. I live in Maryland on this side of Frederick, just across the river."

"Your papers look correct; I will get you a sandwich or two and an apple. Jim, please let him have all he can drink from the well while I prepare his food. Then you can give him a ride as far as Gainesboro or Cross Junction if you can. I believe that is all we can do."

"Thank you both so much. I was not at all certain of my welcome, but afraid I would collapse before getting home. I appreciate your help! My Mother will pray for you."

"No problem, I will be right back. After your drink have a seat on the porch."

When she had finished getting his food and a sandwich and drink for Jim, he was taken in the buggy by the back road to head north. Getting back to the farm into the night, Big Jim was surprised to see that the Misses was still up and had his supper warm.

She told him it was no trouble and she had just cleaned up the kitchen, while she was antsy waiting for his return. It was late of the night as she had expected. She didn't know why but certainly the intrusion of unknowns and her missing men should account for her nervousness. Staff had watched her with caution before they went to bed as instructed. She wasn't ever mean to them but they were always wondering what she would come up with next to be done.

Big Jim was flabbergasted and told her she needed her rest. She laughed and said it was all right she wanted to be certain he came back safely and knew he would be hungry. As he left for the bunk house after eating, he again realized how lucky they all were to be at HER house.

Meanwhile Mildred continued worrying about her "men" and prayed Raymond and Robert would be back soon. She found several other things to do in her room like realigning the clothes in her closet, straightening the dresser drawers, putting clean sheets on the bed, restoking the coals in the fireplace, and generally doing anything she could find that wouldn't wake the household but would keep her from going to bed and having bad dreams about her "men" again!

Maybe tomorrow.....she hoped!

Chapter Three

Mildred had been dreaming – not a good dream either and she sat straight up. It was about searching for Robert and Raymond and about a missing Jim. All craziness of course! She must have been having a nightmare. Her nightgown was twisted around her most uncomfortably and her hair in a giant tangle. She remembered finally that Jim had returned last night as expected. But it was still the other two that were not here! According to the old folks, nightmares were fore bingers of danger. Dear Lord, what else could go wrong! If she did not hear from Raymond this day, she would go to the newspaper office and the rail station and start an official inquiry about him, herself – indeed she would! Plus, anywhere else she thought of when she got her senses back from such a puzzling sleep. She would also see if Mr. Johnson had any further information on the cadets, maybe they had moved again or something. She had to know where her men were! She was valiantly trying to get the knots out of her hair…oh my that hurt! She slipped a dress on and decided she "would do" but knew she wasn't at her best. After adding a clean apron, she heard a lot of talking downstairs.

Mildred remembered Big Jim, her faithful black man from last night, had returned from his escort of the boy. She couldn't imagine the noise was anything untoward regarding the Yankees.

The commotion below stairs continued, she could hear Joshua insisting no one go upstairs and "bother the Missus"!

Now what! She tried her best to make some sense out of her hair once again since they must have company, and using the hog-hair brush, best tortoise shell comb and her fingers got it correct. Slipped the same petticoat as the day before under her dress and made her way downstairs. She was decent but certainly not presentable. She heard more loud talk in the kitchen. A man's voice and then - Raymond's – was it really Raymond?

Being so excited she missed the last step and thankful she was a bit graceful so she didn't fall on her face. It was indeed Raymond and he rushed forward and grabbed her, kissing her soundly in front of all the staff and some man she felt certain she had never seen before. Raymond twirled her around and kissed her again – she was blushing dark red she was certain. Then coming in the door was none other than Robert – he looked startled to see his parents in an arm-lock and then grinned followed by a deep laugh! He was limping and thin as a rail but really looked all right for the most part. He had outgrown his uniform showing a lot of boot and wrists, except in the waist which hung on him. But he was so tall!

She managed to kiss Raymond for about the sixth time and then went and hugged her son. He immediately sat down in a chair and removed his boot. His sock was red with blood and a couple drops dripped on the kitchen floor.

In the meantime, the three guard dogs were sniffing the other man she didn't know. Next the dogs were licking and accepting samples of meat from Robert. Apparently they had acknowledged the guest as part of the family, taking their instruction from the attitude of the rest of them…but they had examined the young man carefully. Not being used to an animal in the house and THREE big ones at that, Alfred was hesitant to pet them at first, but after several licks with sticky tongues, he realized they were being very friendly. However, he also thought they could probably be a force to be reckoned with if aggravated for they were quite muscular and very large compared to the dogs he was used to.

"Oh, God, Robert, Dear! Here take off that dirty sock. Julia bring me a deep basin with good warm water and the bar of lye soap, then burn that awful sock. Mary find me a stack of clean towels and small cloths. Raymond, find the salve and the good bandages…in the upstairs cabinet in the north corner of our bedroom. Also bring that pair of white socks you have…they should be in your dresser drawer and very clean because being white I wash them with the hot water and lye soap Robert put your foot in this basin of hot water – that's the way, now keep it steady – this may hurt."

"Oh, I am sorry, I haven't greeted your friend. Hello, I am Mildred. Please have a seat. Do not mind the dogs, they are friendly to anyone we accept. It is only strangers they wish to devour for their lunch!

Mary now you have brought that, please find out what refreshment our guest would like and also bring something for Raymond and Robert. I am quite beside myself with happiness but also need to see to this foot…it looks septic." Although quite excited and breathless she still noticed the deep blush on Mary's face as she tended to the refreshments for the guest – a young fellow about Robert's age and quite handsome in an underfed way.

"Mother, calm down! My foot is septic but not in too bad a shape, Father stopped by the Reeds' house in Albemarle. They had some damage from the fighting in their very yard, like a couple broken windows, a mini-ball in the wall and so forth but they bathed my foot and also used lye, so it isn't as bad as it may look. You will be glad to know none of their family was killed. This is Captain Alfred Richards, Mother. He and I have suffered through the fighting together. Sitting back-to-back to watch for the enemy at night and managing to stay alive during each day, while commanding our units. Oh, I made captain too but lost my insignia. Enough of that for now – but we are most hungry. Father did stop and get us bread and meat at a store. They were out of tea but provided milk and coffee. Mary are there any cookies? I could eat my weight in cookies. I haven't had any in it seems months on end. Alfred wouldn't you like cookies too?"

Poor Alfred looked like he was quite out of his element. Finally laughing he assured the very red-faced Mary that he would indeed love cookies of any kind and somewhat to drink - anything she wanted to provide, water would be fine or milk or tea or coffee would taste good.

Mary immediately put down plates, a platter of fried ham, platter of fried potatoes, and a dish of scrambled eggs – stating they had been kept warm for Mildred to come down. She added she was grilling hot cakes from the batter she had also made a little while ago. Please eat all they wanted, there was more of everything, plus, syrup and beverages. Then looking alarmed she ran into the dining room and opened the ice box – retrieving a bowl of fruit salad.

"My word, Robert, what a feast! I never dreamed when you said they would rustle up something to eat that it would be a banquet! Thank you, Ma'am! And you too Mr. Adams. I will try to be polite but this is the most food we've seen in quite some time! And fresh butter, too! When did we last have butter, Robert – I can't remember."

"You boys eat all you want. We can provide more of any of that. Both Mary and Julia can cook and know where everything is. What kind of preserves or jelly do you want on your hot cake or bread? There is all the butter and milk you could need, oh, and one bottle of maple syrup left I believe. Our Bossy is a great cow and gives generously each day for milk and cream. Plus, we have two young ones now who were fresh last year and provide good dairy things too. I guess you haven't met the new cows and calves, Son. Oh, and we even have plenty of mulberry or blueberry syrup." While describing the food she continued to work on her son's foot, although difficult with him trying to eat at the same time.

"Anything at all, Ma'am. Anything."

"Well, I want the blueberry, please. I have dreamed about the blueberry syrup all the while I've been gone." Replied Robert. "Mother, when we have eaten, if you don't mind would you look at Alfred's side? He has been bleeding the whole way home and although we don't think the mini-ball is still in him – it appeared to go straight through - it hasn't healed correctly. Very fortunate it didn't hit anything vital like a lung or such. Alfred don't mind Mother checking on your injury, she is quite adept at nursing skills!"

"Of course, I shall, Dear, but let him eat somewhat first." said his mother. "We'll provide him with the blue spare bedroom across from your father's and mine. Some long-johns and means to wash with warm water and soap – Mary - get wash rags and clean towels, too. Then when he has washed himself and is dressed in the long-johns, I will tend to his injury. It should get a good clean first. I will apply lye soap – uncomfortable but the best to get at any infection. We will take good care of you Alfred."

"Oh, thank you, Ma'am! I hate to be a bother but Robert insisted I come home with him. I am from Alexandria so days away from my uncle's home with no horse but have no immediate family remaining. My Mom died when I was in early school and my Father just before the war. So, I am quite alone. I have the property and my uncle rents it for me, but I really have no home to go to. Of course, my uncle would allow me to live with them, but with six children – I am not at all certain it would be a restful place to be!" and he laughed.

"Six children? You are joking aren't you?"

"No, I am not. One is the child of her sister. Both her sister and the husband were killed in a carriage wreck but she and my Uncle took in the child. The rest are theirs. But you wouldn't know which was which or I should say who was who. They have taken the orphan in without blinking an eye. Everyone gets along just fine. It is a little girl and almost the same age as one of their two daughters, so it is three girls and three boys. I must say I admire my aunt and uncle. They handle such a brood with no issues. I would like to marry at some time but don't believe I have the patience for so many youngsters!"

"My parents had wanted a large family but I am the only child. I hope when I marry to have a couple at least – my Mother will be elated!" Said Robert.

"Do you have a girl in mind?"

"Not that I want to say. There is a girl I have met but we'll see. The war intervened and I never asked her to church or to walk out or anything. We'll talk about it later." And Alfred noticed that Robert blushed. In passing he wondered if it was the nice little girl working in the kitchen. He had seen them both blushing a lot. Good to have a girl who knew her way around such an estate. So much to do in a country property like this. Being a city fellow, he had never needed to know how to do so many things but here it would be a full day's work every day he imagined.

The morning progressed with a lot of cooking and eating. It was amazing how young men could devour so much food! Mary was beyond happy! She had no notion that a young man, like Robert, with so much property and education would be interested in HER, but it was such a pleasure to see him again. He was her ideal as a perfect man…kind, generous and hard-working…all the things she knew were important. She had thought of him a lot all the years he was gone to school and the awful war. Praying God would keep him safe and she would see him again. He was just as handsome and personable as ever, although much thinner. She would pray he liked her but knew she was out of his league. Why he could marry someone very rich with lots of property – like Angelina Thomas. He wouldn't need to look at a housemaid like her! But oh, how she admired him! He was smart, kind, handsome, generous, well-educated and handsome (oh, she'd already listed that!)

Chapter Four

The following morning, as things settled down and the "boys", as Miss Mildred called them, were bandaged and resting in rocking chairs near the stove, Mary heard the dogs start to growl. Everyone's head turned toward the front door.

The girls did not look terribly alarmed, but Alfred was. What in tarnation?! Such a noise and all three had their hackles up. It was quite alarming. He had never experienced trained guard dogs before. Country or town dogs who would bark at a stranger, sure, but these fellows acted like they wanted to tear someone apart!

Raymond went immediately and looked out. He pet the dogs and told them they were "good boys". He didn't open the door but as the two strangers came up on the porch the dogs went berserk! Such growling and barking as would deafen the listeners!

The noise of the dogs didn't deter the strangers and one knocked soundly on the door. Raymond asked who it was without opening it. The reply came: "We are officers of the Northern Regiment and want to inspect the premises."

"You will do nothing of the kind! There is no law north or south that gives you a right to enter my home. You move along or I will see you do!"

"Open this door to us! We need to inspect your home for contraband or escaped prisoners."

Without saying another word through the door, Raymond pointed to the dogs and said "GO!" All three very large dogs immediately set up such a racket as Alfred had never heard and even the girls in the kitchen looked alarmed. When the intruders didn't leave the porch, Raymond opened the door. Without a by-your-leave all three huge dogs stormed onto the porch and knocked down the intruders. One on each of them standing on the chest of each culprit and growling fiercely. They didn't bite but it was evident their claws in their feet probably felt awful on the chests of the two men. The third dog, a smaller version of the others, circled, continuing to growl and snarl strongly.

"Get them off! Get them off! They are killing us!"

Behind Raymond, Alfred noticed neither the girls nor the black men seemed concerned.

"They have not even bitten you - yet! They are NOT killing you! But they can! They are trained for protection. We are isolated here and they act on my command or that of my wife or my man servant. You will not be alive by tomorrow if you move. Joshua, please stand guard on these two and do not recall the dogs. Big Jim please ride for the constable. I believe he is at the springs this morning – he was to rest there when we passed him last night. If not, you may need to go to town for someone. Please explain we have intruders. If a sheriff isn't there, get a deputy or an officer of the Northern Army."

"Yes, Master Adams! Right away, Sir! Here Joshua, take this extra gun."

With that the two on the floor of the porch, groaned, but that was not too smart for it set the dogs to loud growling again!

During all this fracas. Alfred was standing back and observing. Never in his born days had he seen such an action. Why those dogs were the best trained he had ever encountered and he was certain the men lying on the porch were not official. He had observed Yankees at the Reid house but none had acted anything like these two. It was obvious to him, as it appeared it was to Mr. Adams that the two were thieves and hoping to get access to the property by pretending to be on Yankee assignment. Any official investigation would show paperwork and have authorized information – probably also accompanied by a local official or sheriff, not to mention clean and repaired uniforms!

Meanwhile, Mildred was carrying on as normal with hardly a glance at the porch. Another thing that amazed him. Robert's mother then told him to go upstairs to the first bedroom on the left. He would find warm water, soap, clean towels and so forth. Please remove yesterday's bandage and clean up his injured area first, then wash the rest of himself as needed and put on the clean new underwear and linsey-woolsey pants laid on the bed. When the clothes had been laid out he had no idea but saw another girl he hadn't met coming down the same stairs. Evidently Mrs. Adams had been giving all instructions while he had been enthralled with the excitement on the porch.

Wow what a turn-around! He couldn't wait to tell his uncle about his visit here and all the excitement…not sure he would be believed but he knew it had actually happened - he certainly wasn't dreaming!

About the time he was thoroughly washed and dressed in the woolsey pants, there was a knock and upon invitation Mrs. Adams entered with Mary. She spread a small coverlet on top of the bedspread and told him to lie down and pull the waist of the pants below his injury as he had done the day before. He had noticed when he removed yesterday's bandage and washed how angry it looked and was still oozing a red and yellowish blood. Mildred Adams set about cleaning it thoroughly as before, while the girl handed her fresh rags she had soaped with the lye, putting soiled ones in a bucket also by the bed.   He tried not to cry out but it hurt like the very devil much as yesterday! The two women continued bothering him with the lye until they seemed satisfied they had the area very clean. Then taking a thick greenish-yellow substance, Mrs. Adams applied it to the whole open area. He was braced for it to hurt again but it really did not – feeling cool and tingly but not the burning pain of the cleaning procedure. She then applied several layers of a gauze fabric and told him to hold it on and stand up. As he did so she eased his pants down a little further and took strips of cloth and wound them around his hips to hold the medicine and gauze in place. More bandage than yesterday – maybe she felt it wouldn't need disturbing so soon again. Fastening it quite tightly. She then told him to carefully pull up the pants and make certain he did not let the bandage slip off the injury. She added she had left some more of the bandage and he could wind it around the wound and around the upper part of his leg and then tie it off if needed. She apologized that she had nothing sticky to use but had wound the gauze in a pattern that should hold all right as long as he didn't disturb it overmuch. She had slit the last few feet of the rest of the wrapping and tied it around his thigh. Alfred nodded that he understood and thanked her profusely. It was embarrassing to have two women that he barely knew working on his almost naked body but appreciated that it was for his benefit for sure and certain!

He noticed as he tried to walk downstairs the bandage wanted to move, so he returned to the bedroom and rewound part of the extra bandage overtop of his thigh under the long johns, taking it through his crotch and finally around his waist to tie it. That seemed to hold better. He would ask for some more of the strips later and fasten them again around his waist and leg more securely. Going back down, the two reprobates were still on the porch and whenever one would move an eyelash one of the dogs would growl. What great beasts they were – the dogs that is! Neither of the men was going anywhere.

When he got to the kitchen table, Robert was talking with Mary and blushing like a school-boy. Good for him, she seemed like a nice and capable girl and was indeed very good looking. Both boys, at Mary's invitation, ate some more of today's delicious breakfast.

Alfred dozed in front of the stove until the other girl, Julia, tapped shyly on his arm and asked if he could please move his chair she needed to use the oven. He apologized and assisted her to load a huge baking pan with a large ham in it. Oh boy, would that taste good!

They had enjoyed a beef stew the night before but ham was his favorite. Someone had sliced lines in the fat covering and put preserves and dark sugar on the top too. He was amazed the slight girl could lift the huge pan but she seemed to manage well. On the back of the stove, he saw too pots with steam coming out of them. When he asked, Julia responded that one was potatoes and the other would be corn on the cob for their luncheon, the ham was for supper later. Tonight, they would have creamed peas too – the last of the fresh peas for this year and fried apples, which the "Master" really liked when there was ham. They had already baked the ham for several hours but would need to bake one hour more with the sweetness and dried cloves on top. He had no idea what fried apples would taste like feeling certain he had never eaten anything like that – applesauce he had at home but never a "fried" apple.

Alfred moved his chair to the side, out of the way and just before he dozed off again marveled that they had great food last evening, and today a huge breakfast, would have steak for lunch, and ham for supper! He then happily slept. He was awakened somewhat later by a commotion on the porch. Getting up he noticed out the window there were three –

really three – men in Yankee uniforms and talking sternly to the men on the porch. Master Adams was putting the three dogs back in the house, although all three looked like it was supper time outside and don't move them! These same dogs that had licked his hand and sat by his chair when he was just introduced to them yesterday were actively growling and looking like they could make supper out of the strange errant men, now tied up, on the porch. Amazing! He wondered how anyone could train such big beasts to be so selective in their choice of who to bite and who not.

Mildred came up to him. "I see you admiring our beasts! I love those three dogs. Aren't they something…they know who to like and who to try to bite. Had those men hurt one of us, I am most certain they would have done serious damage to such people until called off by Raymond or myself or Joshua. I have no idea how Raymond trained them so easily. But it didn't take him much time when each was a puppy. He had gotten instruction from Germany, where such dogs have been trained for years. He had done the same since a boy and we have helped neighbors train as well. It includes rationing their food and teaching them commands with rewards when correct – such as a piece of steak. Of course, it takes a certain temperament and breeding in the dogs. I don't know that just any dog can be trained that severely. Trained to bark or growl on command probably, but I seriously believe these would actually attack if necessary."

"Oh, I agree, Ma'am, I agree. Their very demeanor is of serious protection. You must feel safer having them here."

"I do indeed. I am not a person to be easily afraid. During this war, I have turned away those I did not feel deserved help but the dogs are such a blessing. We are affluent and attract 'ner'do'wells looking for an easy take. Well, I will cut a beef steak from the side in the icehouse for them tonight. They deserve it!"

Laughing, Alfred said a beef steak was a good reward...it had been months and months since he had eaten such. Thinking to himself he would be happy to not see another dish of dried beans or corn cakes!

Shortly thereafter the intruders were "escorted" from the property by the soldiers and peace again reigned on the front porch. When the dogs came back into the house there was no obvious animosity toward Joshua nor Alfred nor anyone else. Their job was over and they knew not to worry further…a real study in animal behavior, which had always interested him. He had often thought he would like to work with animals, such as training horses but maybe he would also try dogs….very interesting afternoon indeed!

His nap over, Alfred had found the kitchen smelled delicious! Looking at the stove, there were now enough beef steaks grilling on the iron burners for everyone! Mrs. Adams had heard his comment he bet. Steak for luncheon. Oh, my. How had he ever been so lucky as to end up here! Evidently the ham was indeed for supper.

The afternoon continued to be interesting. He managed, after eating all he could hold, the dinner would be something to look forward to. He would walk to the barn – inspecting the new cows and calves as well as the faithful older ones. They were obviously the pride of Robert, for the new additional animals had arrived during his absence. Robert had managed the walk with some difficulty. As they finished their barn tour, including brushing the horses, and inspecting an apparatus that Henry Thomas had shown them how to construct. It had tines on a semi-circular wooden piece, controlled by a long handle that made the spikes take a portion of the over-head stored hay and it would fall into the stalls below. They would remove just enough of this upper hay to feed without having to climb a ladder and fork it down. This new contraption would then be moved along until it was over the next stall of animals. The black man named Big Jim had come and brought a hand cart and insisted Robert not try to walk back to the house, that he would push him. Now how thoughtful was that! Such a successful place and everyone working together so well. Alfred was learning a lot. He certainly was. He thanked the man, who had offered to come back for him, but refused and continued his walk saying he needed to move.

Upon being delivered to the house by Big Jim, Robert reflected on his attraction to Mary. He had thought about her often during school and the war. She was a good student in primary school, therefore smart, attended church, she handled many of the jobs around the estate, therefore capable, and she certainly was attractive! Thinking of that he wondered if Alfred would be interested in her. Although not ready to ask for her hand in marriage, he was just returning after four years – but maybe it would be good to let his friend know he was interested in Mary and to not get any ideas of courting her himself.

Yup, that was what he would do. He had to be certain his injury would not cripple him and that he was set to take over his share of the farm or purchase more acreage, but still never hurt to be prepared.

He would talk to his parents soon. If he lived here, then he would have a share in their farm – of course helping everywhere, but maybe they would not want that. They had never talked about his future here. Or just a cursory – "When you grow up." He would talk to them soon. The more he was around Mary the more he was thinking of marriage. Well, why not, he had finished his education and was of an age to do so…Oh, Mary I wonder if you would consider it?

Fleetingly he surmised about what Alfred's plans were. He hoped his good friend would settle in this area. While not used to farming, Alfred had stated a couple times the last few days that it interested him a lot. How nice it would be for them to stay close friends and work together. Hopefully Alfred would marry – but not to his girl – no siree!

He thought of one more civil war note, word had been received at the telegraph office and delivered to a few of the homes where soldiers resided, by Mr. Johnson. It was heart breaking in that it told of many, many hundreds of Rebels and Yankees killed and a large victory for the Northern forces. The battle at Petersburg, Virginia had ended in a bloody onslaught. With a decided win by the Yankees and had been a substantial part of the decision of General Lee to surrender. Robert had known several who had fought there. He prayed for the souls of them all!

Chapter Five

With his side feeling much better Alfred decided to take his time going back to the house and examined the icehouse, the garden, the grainery and so forth. The grainery was interesting – it had big boxy tubs of various grains and long-handled paddles for turning it occasionally. The windows had screens and were open but on the outside were large, hinged overs or flaps that would close each opening if it rained or snowed to keep the grain dry and not let it mold. Quite ingenious! He had little farm information and what ones they had been on during the War hadn't provided much he needed to know - frequently being torn up or his troop was on a march and had no time to stop and learn anything.

He liked the efficiency and the good production. They must sell a lot of field crops, animals, eggs, garden produce, fruit, nuts, grains, and an abundance.

Even with the eight or nine employees he had seen – and there were probably lots more for fieldwork – they seemed to raise huge numbers of animals, grains, and vegetables. Even the chicken coops were long and he hadn't looked about sheep and hogs yet but knew from talking with Robert that there were both.

He would really like to farm. It would be a gigantic learning experience, but he was certain Robert would help him. He had never been much of a city dweller. It was alright to go to an occasional card party or musical performance, but he would much rather farm. His uncle had encouraged him to study the law, which he had done a little at VMI until the war intervened but that held no interest either. There was some rental property that was his, but just town property for rent – no acreage or farms.

On his way back to the house he went in the direction of the chicken coops and also to look at the orchards a bit…he was getting tired so he would not tour the whole thing but he was interested in seeing as far as his worn and injured body would take him this evening.

Suddenly he saw something along the fence line that bordered the lane. What in tarnation was that? Why had someone thrown out a bunch of laundry or old clothes? He was quite certain Mrs. Adams would be much more efficient with the use of those things. He would go and take what he could carry back to the house and inquire.

He stumbled along, getting more tired with each tread but when he got close he was so alarmed he turned and ran – shouting as loudly as he could. He was stumbling in his exhaustion but knew he had to alert someone! If it wasn't a dead body then it was someone close to being such. Finally Big Jim seemed to notice him and came running at full speed toward him. "Sir, Sir, what do you need? Sir, please, slow you down! You will do damage to your wound!" As breathless as he was he managed to croak that "there is a man back there".... And pointed toward the fence row.

Big Jim nodded and passed him at a pace Alfred was certain he couldn't have run when he was in a perfect state of body and health! He heard Jim blow a whistle – quite a loud blast.

About that time another young black man, whose name had escaped Alfred, maybe Ray, came on horseback and asked did he need a ride to the house, he had been sent to fetch him. Gasping for air, their guest said "No thank you, but you should follow Big Jim. I believe there is a man down or a body along the fence row!" and gasping he flopped down on a piece of log along the lane. "Oh, I thought the whistle was for you. I will be back, Sir, stay here."

Someone from the house must have been watching the turn-around and Master Raymond Adams came running accompanied by one of the dogs. Not long thereafter another black man that Alfred didn't know came on horseback leading a second animal for the master to mount – which he did. Stopping by Raymond, he inquired if he was all right and Alfred assured him he was but just breathless, so Raymond continued on toward the others. The dog had given him a cursory glance but was more interested in what was ahead in the lane. He watched as Raymond dismounted and got down on his knees beside the pile of clothes along the fence. The dog barked several times, not an angry bark but seemingly an "alert" type of noise.

The unknown black came racing back on his horse and turned toward the carriage shed. In short order he had the horse properly reigned and attached to a buggy and was taking it at great speed back toward the same fence area. Their guest continued to observe the whole procedure and from the way they handled the "person" in the rags, it was obvious that they thought him alive. Placing the person carefully in the small carriage and Raymond getting in as well and holding the head and shoulders. Seconds later the whole contraption came racing back toward the house. Mildred was at the gate holding it open so the black driver could aligned the buggy properly with the porch. She must have seen part of the action from the kitchen windows. Another one of the dogs barked a warning but not consistent noise while Mildred and Janice, the upstairs maid, assisted by Joshua, gently progressed with the carrying of the "person" who had lain along their road. Raymond then got out and gave instructions to one of the men to remove the carriage evidently – for within minutes it was back in the lane and headed for him.

What a day! Amazing how efficient the whole procedure had been after he had alerted them. With his breath back he managed to stumble or almost crawl into the buggy but with less difficulty than he might have imagined. He was glad for the ride back up the lane and to the porch steps. A concerned Robert asked if he was all right, he had been gone a long time. He assured him he was exhausted but really quite all right and felt the bandage on his side under the shirt but there was no moisture so he thought he had not reopened his wound.

He was glad to see Robert's mother in action. Mildred Adams was a picture of organization! They had the fellow disrobed and in bed before Alfred Richards got back in the house. Mary was assisting Mildred and the two women had obviously done the like before – there was not a wasted movement and fresh hot water, soap, clean rags, blankets and salves were produced immediately and spread on a small table that had been pushed up to the bedside. A girl he had seen in the kitchen came up with a tray with beaker and tea pot and such.

The saved man appeared quite young, had blonde hair, and was badly soiled and bruised as observed from the doorway. Alfred continued on to "his" room, flopping down with a sigh. Well, he had exercised far too much, that was certain, but what a day it had been! The farm had provided many things of interest and he knew it would probably be financially possible to purchase a farm of his own.

Not this huge size but large enough to support a family. Many who had such may have either given up farming or were killed or injured whereby the heirs would be selling property. He would put his money to good use. If he could find something in this part of the state it would please him no end. He loved looking at the blue mountains, the friendliness of the people, and the good soil.

He got up and walked to the door to glance once more down the hall at the other room with the invalid. Raymond was just leaving with the dirty rags the man had worn – probably to burn them. And Julia was coming up with another pitcher of water and a jar of some kind of yellowish-greenish matter –a salve or such like used on him.

Stepping back into his room, he thought he would just rest a few minutes and close his eyes for a bit, but he was sound asleep within seconds. Quite a day for an invalid!

Chapter Six

Alfred had napped and then washed himself and put on a clean shirt of Robert's they had given him. Going downstairs, Julia had inquired if he was all right. He assured her with his dimpled grin that he was indeed – had been quite tired from his expedition but felt much like his old self after his rest. His bandage had stayed in place on his side. He noticed Julia blushed and looked down at the floor. Well, good, he would like her to be aware of him. He thought she was very pretty, kind and energetic. He had seen what good help she was to Mrs. Adams.

Alfred inquired of Raymond about his "find" and was assured the boy did live and that Doctor Weems had come and was still there with him as were his wife and Mary. He felt the boy would continue to live – thanks entirely to Alfred! If he had not noticed or assumed it was just trash and not taken an interest, the doctor said he was most certain the boy would have been dead by morning.

Asking if they knew who he was, Julia and Raymond both said they had no idea. Doctor Weems did not know but thought he had seen him working somewhere but couldn't remember where. It had been when the boy was much younger if the same one. No papers were found in his pocket but the other pocket was torn apart from a shot that had barely missed his body and the uniform further damaged by brambles. Robert also didn't know the boy but thought he looked familiar. It was believed he was younger than they were. It appeared his breeches were Confederate, the rest of his clothing so torn and dirty it was hard to tell if a uniform or not.

He had most likely been shot in the back shoulder, where he couldn't have attended it. He also had scrapes and an ankle so enlarged it was thought a miracle if he could put any weight on it. Possibly a broken bone but Julia didn't know if the doctor had made that decision yet.

Another person in the house was wondering about this unfortunate boy as well. Mildred thought, now they had him washed up, that she had seen him before but for the life of her couldn't remember where. Something in the back of her mind thought he may have worked as a young boy at the grainery or the accompanying store at the springs. They would inquire. Most likely there was at least someone who was missing him.

On a happier note, Mildred had not missed the blush on Julia's face when talking with the Richards boy nor had she missed the excitement of Mary when her Robert was back. Well, how nice. Both girls were just about perfect. They had finished school – meaning they could read and do sums quite well. Which was not always common for working girls, and they could manage a kitchen and knew quite a lot about household chores including some sewing and canning. Mary was adept at sewing and did beautiful embroidery. She was even learning how to make many of the home remedies and salves when it was not possible to buy some – as in mid-winter if snowed in or because of embargos. Time would tell, the "boys" were just back and probably had not encountered many girls or women in their several years at VMI and fighting.

As she turned back to the bed she was pleased to see two very blue eyes looking at her with a confused expression on his face.

"Am I in Heaven? I am sure and certain I was dying. Is this Heaven indeed?"

"No, Dear Boy, it is not Heaven. We have been attending you since you were found in our lane yesterday. I am Mildred Adams and this is my house you are in. Doctor Weems has been helping you and came back today. He has just gone to the kitchen for a bite to eat and cup of tea. Do you think you could swallow some tea, Dear?"

"Oh, yes, Ma'am if you don't mind. I don't want to be a bother but my throat is very dry."

Pouring him a cup from a pitcher on the dresser, she brought it over. "This is tepid, I'm afraid, but let's start with it. I added some sugar, too." She noticed him wince as he tried to rise and told him to not try to raise his shoulder but to just roll on his good side to drink. He followed her instructions well and did gulp down the whole cup. She supported his head as she helped tip the cup.

"Oh, that was nice! I am not certain what day it is but know pretty well that I have not had ought to eat or drink for some days. I did lap some water from a trough and ate a few berries and a couple rotten apples but I have been too far gone to do much else."

"Well, we are all so pleased you made it to our house where we can help you! You must have walked considerable distance to get here for there is no fighting hereabouts."

"Seems I remember being in a cart with several others injured. We were heading as prisoners to the Yankee encampment at Gerrardstown. Someone with a northern accent – like a Yankee - said: "He is dead!" and threw me out. I couldn't speak to tell him I wasn't dead. I lay there quite a while in the brush along a road. Two different horsemen went past but I was laying on my good side and couldn't raise this other arm to hail them.

I started to crawl, as you can probably tell from my knees. I crawled for two days and part of each night, passing out on occasion. I saw what may have been your lane and could tell it was well maintained, so attempted to get to the house assuming someone lived here. That's the last I remember. Where was I found?"

"You are correct it was in our lane. You have Captain Alfred Richards to thank for that. He had been taking a little exercise with his damaged body and saw something he thought was thrown away clothes – it turned out to be you!" and she laughed.

"Oh, Dear, rescued by a Captain. It is almost unbelievable! I must thank him when I am able."

"You will have a chance to do so, he is staying here for quite a while, I imagine. Now I hear Julia coming up the stairs and she will have some soup or such for you. Here, let me put a couple pillows behind you to support that awful shoulder. Dr. Weems has attended it and it will get well, but I realize it must be most uncomfortable for you right now – Doctor did considerable cleaning and stitching. Remember roll to your good side if you need to change position to eat or drink. I have put a waste jar on a stool by your bed for your convenience so you don't have to get out of bed to use a commode jug or outhouse. Oh, Dear, what am I to call you? I don't know your name and we found no papers on you when we took your wet clothes off."

"Oh, Dear, what a terrible bother I am! I apologize for all this extra work! My name is Carlie – Carlie Allen Davis, it may have been Carl but my Mom has been dead these many years and all anyone has called me is Carlie."

"What nonsense! Don't apologize to me! And we will call you Carlie. I could not be more pleased that you will get well and are alert and sensible. You have had a serious ordeal. Once you have eaten something, I will be up with paper, pen and ink. If you give me the name and address of any relative, I will write and let them know you are here and recuperating."

"Oh, you are more than kind, but I have no one. I have been orphaned since I was six and pick up part-time jobs – trying to get ones where they will let me sleep in the hay mow or such and provide me meals for a portion of what I earn. I am afraid I never attended school past the first year and a half. But thank you for the very kind thought."

Mildred almost ran from the room. She could not let the poor child see when she cried. He has no one? Oh, Dear. Well, they could always use another hand and there were still two beds available in the bunk house, which held twelve when full. The beds had mattresses and covers and three meals a day were provided for all who worked on this estate and had no nearby home to travel from. The fireplace there was lit when the weather called for it and many lanterns some with candles and some burning coal oil. Wash basins and slop jars were available and cleaned by the tenants, and outhouse if they preferred. Not at all a bad place to live.

He would be all right – if he wanted to that is. Alice was their girl that came four or five days a week from the village and on her days she took care of the food, washing clothes and bedding for the help and so forth. Mildred would see Alice knew about the addition as soon as his shoulder healed enough for him to move there. Julia would help for she also did some of the work at the bunk house or assigned staff on the weekends or when Alice couldn't come. And Julia or Alice could teach him jobs. As to his education, she had taught Robert to read and do small sums before he even started school. She would teach Carlie too. Three of them would have him reading and doing sums in no time!

When she got downstairs, Raymond asked about the patient and between bouts of crying Mildred explained he had no relatives, that he knew of anyway, and nowhere to go. They would keep him.

Raymond laughed and said he wasn't a piece of furniture they could take possession of. What if he didn't want to stay?

"Well, then I guess when he is well enough to travel, I will just have to let him go…but I don't want to, Dear. He needs a "home" and we can easily provide that."

"We will offer him a home here, Dear. But we can't make him accept it. He has traveled on his own almost his whole life. He may find us too restricting. However, he must be the one to decide." Said her husband.

"Yes. Thank you, Raymond. I agree."

Chapter Seven

The next three weeks at the Adams house were relatively uneventful, given that something needed attention immediately on a regular basis but nothing else untoward had occurred. The three soldiers continued to improve – including the poor boy from the lane who had been mistaken for a pile of trash.

Mildred was her usual efficient self, almost being two places at once and with several servants in her wake trying to keep up with the list of "necessary" things to be found, applied, cooked, cleaned, or otherwise handled. Raymond had gone to the mill and store at the pond several times instead of once a month. The list included the need to replace a goodly number of jars and flagons used to donate food, medicines, or give to passersby. They were expensive but he knew Mildred wouldn't have given any away unnecessarily. He purchased a number of other things, some for the ailing, some to replace medical supplies Mildred liked to have on hand, and to get some treats for the three young men – like chocolate, plus vanilla beans, or cinnamon to use to make various cookies including of course cinnamon/raisin cookies. Mildred was glad they had dried a lot of grapes the year before, because Robert and the two "guests" seemed to be able to devour raisin cookies by the dozens.

It was quite noticeable that Robert and Mary seemed interested in each other. Mary was shy but from her blush and stumbling around when he complimented her – she gave her feelings away. Mildred hadn't thought a lot about him getting married – first he had school, then VMI and "with God Help Us" the war. But they had always been friends and that is a good start. As he hobbled about trying to help her that was a good sign too. Twice he had the start of infection again in the foot but the last four days it was very much better. Mildred had helped Alfred with his side and it was healing very well now, too. Poor Carlie was still having a lot of trouble with the shoulder and accompanying huge wound on his back. Doctor Weems had come a couple more times and they kept it clean and bandaged but it was so deep and such a long cut that the doctor felt it would be a month before it improved a lot. No infection this week though! And Doctor

Weems felt he would not lose the arm or need any other such serious surgery. Mildred didn't take any credit but Raymond knew it was her constant care of the wound that had done it. A couple times he had helped hold the boy almost upside down while she attended the raw area. - much to the embarrassment of Carlie.

Alfred had started talking a lot to Julia and she likewise seemed to look after him at meals and so forth. He had written to his uncle several times about this farm and gotten correspondence back. The uncle, aunt and six cousins had been invited by Mildred to come and visit and they had agreed. One of the things she had her "girls" doing was getting the three spare bedrooms on the third story cleaned and bedding washed in the event his relatives did come for a visit. Usually, the two large extra rooms on the second floor would suffice, but with the injured "boys", those were not available. They also had laid a fire a couple times in each of the top floor three bedrooms. Someone always watched it to be certain the chimney on that end of the house was drawing correctly and wouldn't belch smoke all over the place. Alfred's aunt had written to Mildred a couple times and with replies there was little left that one didn't know about the other.

For two days Raymond had been in town, staying the night at their cousin Jessie's house so he could testify to the intrusion and fake identification used by the two unwelcome "visitors" that his dogs had so greatly kept in tow until the Yankee military police had taken them off. During the trial it was found that they had pulled the same trick on others, two successful and two not. Mildred did not want to think what the military tribunal would sentence them to…it would be very harsh, even though perpetrated on the property of a Confederate.

All three "boys" had wanted to go but were discouraged. Raymond felt his testimony would be enough and probably not an advantage to have any former Confederate soldiers in the mix – it was now considered a national court and rules were still pretty strict about any of the defeated Confederates taking part – however Mildred felt they were lucky that the Yankees did arrest the two. Personally, they had experienced little trouble with the Yankee overseers and on occasion shared some treat, like cookies or fruit cake with the ones stationed at Gerardstown. (Pronounced = gerits/town). Raymond didn't like it but she said the war was over and they would have to live together, so share she would!

Robert studied his Mother more than he ever had. She had always been a power to be reconned with but the more he observed her: her good sense, friendly manner and generosity; he realized how very fortunate he was. He couldn't have picked better from hundreds and she kept the estate in pristine condition. Plus, her good works were known all over the area. Now that he got to town or the mill on occasion, he was continually having people tell him how wonderful she was and she had brought such and such a food when it was scarce or given such and such a medication, even provided homemade quilts to some of the black families in the area. When he would ask about anything like that she would brush it off and say they exaggerated. But he didn't believe that for a minute!

All three of the boys had been mustered out of the army – an army that no longer existed but they had papers now to show they had served and were legally excused. Raymond felt that General Lee was a good man and had fallen into leading the Confederacy because of his intelligence and training. However, it had cost him dearly. All his lands were taken. Thankfully on the request of the Union Generals and President Lincoln (before he was assassinated of course), he was not incarcerated.

Things were looking good on the farm. They had purchased the huge field to the west of them from their neighbor's wife, Olivia Horn. Mr. Horn had passed away two years ago and because Mildred had attended him and been a constant help to his widow, they were named a price for the property that they couldn't refuse. It did provide more land for crops, having been fertilized, weeds turned under, and plowed for these many years. With Robert home, he could repay his parents for it and the land would give him a place closer to their house and a huge field he could call his own and raise whatever he desired – sort of a starter farm – along with helping at the big one. He had mentioned maybe using it at least partially for sweet corn and his father had agreed that was a good idea. A most popular crop and they had all the equipment for behind the horse that would be needed to plant it. The land was really large enough that a nice home could be built on the section that had a rise and would overlook Little North Mountain and the nearby farms. So, options were available.

As Mildred took a break from wash day, she was gazing out the front window and watching the breeze stir the flowers and contemplating on how much she loved this farm, when she noticed two horsemen riding up the lane toward the house. She turned and whistled for the dogs. It may be friends and if so, then fine. But if not, she would be prepared. Several homes had been broken into lately plus things like wagons and buggies stolen. She was not one to take chances.

Raymond, Robert and Alfred had ridden to town for a number of things, like haircuts – probably tired of her cutting around a crock placed over their head. They would get medicines not available at the mill, and to buy newspapers with the latest information regarding the reconstruction. (Reconstruction being changes to the laws and other requirements from "Federal" courts as the results of the civil war). Joshua was helping raise a new section to the barn and would be too far away to see the lane. Tarnation! Well, she had the dogs and Big Jim was out at the icehouse cleaning it up…He should hear her if she called out the upstairs window. Not to panic…wait and see what was about.

As the horsemen got closer to the gate all three dogs went on the alert. "Good Boys!" She told them. There were low grumbles and hackles had started to rise. Obviously they were not known to visit for the dogs hackles never rose when someone came they had met. They would bark if it wasn't a "regular" but not be on attentive alert. Now they were on alert for sure and certain! She got her pistol and loaded it and brought two rifles into the kitchen. Mary had heard the dogs and came downstairs from her work on the third story rooms – which were almost finished.

"Mary, Dear, run up to the bedroom over the kitchen and open the window and call for Big Jim, who is working on the icehouse, to come immediately, please."

"Yes, Ma'am!" And she ran up the stairs beside the kitchen storage safe to the bedroom closest to the icehouse in the back yard. Mildred heard her shrill whistle and a response from Big Jim.

Okay that would get him here for sure and certain.

The interlopers were nearing the gate and had tied their horses and were coming through toward the porch. They wore Union army clothes but dirty and ragged – not like they would look if on official business. The dogs were adamantly growling now with an occasional loud bark and their hackles were up as high as they would go. She felt shivers and told the dogs they were "Good Boys!" again. A loud knocking occurred and someone outside tried to open the door. How dare they. The dogs went crazy!

"Open Up! We demand you open this door immediately!"

"No, Sir! Not until you identify yourselves and state your business. I am armed and have three trained attack dogs. I do not recommend you try to enter my home!"

"We will arrest you, Ma'am. You must obey the law. Open up immediately!"

"I am not aware of any law that makes me allow you into my home, Sir. You need to explain yourselves and show your papers of authority at my window."

There was much muttering on the porch and the dogs continued their tirade of barking and intermittent growling. She heard Big Jim enter from the back yard and could hear him also throw the bolts on the back door to the washing room and again on the kitchen door. Mary came back downstairs and had the gun and pistol from the upper wardrobe with her including two boxes of ammunition. Big Jim took them and loaded both. He asked about Mildred's but she explained she had already loaded. She sent Mary to stealthily look out various windows at the end of the house, the music room, the downstairs bedroom windows and any back window – maybe even going up to the bedrooms both on the second and third floors, where she could look down and around better. "Please tell Carlie to not worry but leave him a gun and ammunition – one of those Big Jim just loaded. Try to see if only the two horsemen are on the property or if there are others surrounding the house, Dear. Also, in the third-floor wardrobe are a rifle and another old one-shot pistol but bring them and any ammunition too please. They may not work but we can try to clean them unless these two knock the door down right away or come in a window." At saying that, she heard Big Jim make a noise like a growl more than she had ever heard him do before.

One of the dogs took off for the dining room. Evidently one of the men had gone in that direction on the porch with the intent to try to get in a window or the parlor door. Mildred heard a noise behind her and there stood Carlie – gun in hand. "I will defend the lower rooms, Ma'am. I am a good shot. I didn't see a lot of action in the service but I can handle a gun just fine. Do not worry, I am all right. My back hurts but not terribly – I am perfectly capable to help defend!" And he went through the dining room and down the half flight in the direction of the music room. After letting Mildred know she had seen nothing untoward out the windows, Mary, loaded rifle in hand, stationed herself out of sight but with an aim through the dining room window. They would not enter that way with her there and she didn't believe in the dark room they would see her to fire directly at her either. She had never shot a person but had learned to hunt while still a girl at home and she was an excellent shot. She had hunted deer and squirrels. She wished Julia wasn't off with her family today… she also is a good shot. And what a day for all three men to be in town! She wondered fleetingly if the culprits had watched and seen the men leave.

Mildred had no idea how well-armed the vagrants were, having not actually seen them up close while she was busy organizing this defense. She also hoped there were no others!

Extremely hard knocking was heard at the door with the command to "Open Up!!" again. She ignored the demand. She didn't want to respond and let them know

where she was by her voice. The dogs'
noise was deafening! All three were
loudly barking.

Suddenly the youngest dog ran to the side
kitchen window and barked...not his
usual alert bark but more a greeting!
How very strange! What in the world!
Seconds later there was a quiet tap on the
washroom door. Big Jim went unlocked
the kitchen and demanded at the laundry
door who was there. Then opened it.
Mildred had not heard who answered.
Looking over her shoulder, there came
Joshua! Thank Heaven!

"Oh, Joshua! I am so glad you knew to
come! How many are there, could you
tell?"

"I only saw the two on the porch and
there was only Big Jim's footprint in the
mud at the back door. I think we can
handle them with little difficulty. Wait
until they enter, you have the law on your
side if you shoot them in your home!"

Of course, a former slave would know
that. How grand to have such good

defense. She heard a gun bolt thrown and got down behind the wall whistling for the two remaining dogs to join her, the other dog was still growling in the dining room. Joshua turned the kitchen table on its side and formed a shield in case they knocked the door down and entered.

A hard thump and broken glass was heard at the dining room window – just like Mildred had understood was done at Nancy Hendricks house one time by deserters during the war, when Nancy's son had fired and killed a reprobate entering there. Of course, dining room windows were subject to entrance being along the porch and usually just glass to admit as much light as possible. A shot rang out and from the loud noise Mildred didn't know whether it was inside or out. Joshua immediately left the protection of the upset table and rushed to check on Mary in the dining room.

Mary was looking at her gun as if she had never seen it before and then pointed to the window. Joshua didn't see anything at first but cautiously walked around the broken glass and looking out saw a man lying on the porch holding his shoulder.

"Good shot, Little Missy! Good shot!"

"You on the porch – do NOT move! That is the first shot you have received but certainly not the last if you move at all! I have a gun on you too and I will also shoot."

He could see that the other man had crawled toward the dining room window but evidently to only see to his companion.

"Robbie, oh Robbie! Are you badly hurt? Let's go! They have us outnumbered and we need to leave. Can you make it to our horses?"

"Yes, Tim, I can. If they don't shoot me again!"

"Leave your weapons right there on the porch. Leave them, I said! Now go – both of you – GO!"

Hearing the heavy male voice with no black accent, they didn't realize it was a former slave giving the orders. How funny was that thought Mary amid her fright and exhaustion.

As the two managed to get on their horses, leaving their rifles behind as ordered, there was the sound of hoofbeats coming down the lane. Joshua unlatched the door and ran out. He shouted for their men to stop the fleeing criminals.

Hours later, the sheriff and two federal men were leaving with two prisoners. Their men explained finally that they had a "funny" feeling on their trip and after hearing there were two escaped Federal prisoners about in the White Hall direction, they started back for home.

Meanwhile, Big Jim had found a new piece of glass the correct size in the grainery and was replacing the dining room window with Mary holding strips of wood to be nailed to hold it in place.

Well past supper time, a meal was finally ready and the very tired people all sat down together to eat. It was nice having young Carlie at the table with them and per Mildred's inspection, he had not done any damage to his shoulder at the back.

Big Jim and Joshua had been invited to dinner too but elected to take a large portion of the baked ham offered by Mildred out to the men in the bunkhouse. With Joshua then going up to his home, where his wife would have food prepared. Meanwhile Mildred was frying three chickens – hard to tell how much food was needed for such hungry men – but better more than not enough.

It had been a most exhausting day. But what a good group they were, thought Mildred. All working so well together and Mary was such a fine shot. Mildred told Robert all about Mary's brave action and he complimented her profusely as she blushed three shades of red.

After dinner Mildred noticed the two young people went into the parlor by themselves. Alfred winked at her and so she figured her son was probably going to ask Mary to wed. How nice! They were both quite mature and had been through a lot. A good pair for certain! And Robert now had that extra land to use. He had probably bought her a ring while in town today. Meanwhile, Alfred also was talking quietly with Julie – my goodness love bloomed large these days. Well, that was good news too. She would miss Julia if they married and moved away, as they most assuredly would, but that was all right too…just as God would wish! The new maid, Alice, was sitting at the table, as invited, but not eating. She looked entirely out of her element. Shooting, cooking, black men all over the place, a building full of workers, and three men who had been injured from the war! Also, more food than she had ever seen in her lifetime. What in the world had she gotten into? And she was invited to eat at the table! Well, she would write to her Mother for certain, but it was also assured that her Mother wouldn't believe it by half!

Little did Alice know that she would be amazed on a regular basis if she stayed employed at this house. For things were always busy and between helping others, running one of the most successful and largest farms in this area, and with the guard dogs it was a most alarming and peculiar place to work – but she was treated very well, better than other places she had been, and the food was spectacular. It would take her many pages to write it all to her mother.

Mildred's guesses had been correct and both young couples had agreed to wed within the next year. Not right away – the men had to plan more for their future – but the promises had been made. On top of that happy news, Big Jim had asked the next morning for a meeting with "the Missus and the Master". Oh, my, she so hoped he wasn't leaving, although all slaves being free now, he had always been free and with them since a very young boy. But of course, he could choose to work elsewhere. What would they do without his good work and care for the animals plus they liked him so much, even as scary as he was!

But it was good news, he too wanted to get married. He said he had been stepping out with Annie King, the girl he sat with at his church at Wadesville. If it was agreeable with the Master and Missus they would like to build a house on the acre he had been promised if he should ever marry just like Joshua had. Was that all right?

Well, it was more than all right! She was a lovely girl and came from an industrious long ago freed black family. They would be very happy, Mildred was certain. Both she and Raymond congratulated him and stated they would provide the materials to build a house and also a wedding feast. They would ask him to get a few of his friends to help with the construction. On that happy note the household planned a reception and discussed what materials to gather for building Big Jim's house. She would think about it and plan a nice place for them.

Chapter Eight

Many couples without wealthy relatives used fireplaces to cook and heat, all had outhouses and few had built-in cabinets. Their beds sometimes only had wooden slats to hold thin mattresses and few extra rooms, cupboards or closets. None of this suited Mildred. She said Big Jim had provided them with the best of work ethic and protection. They would build him a "proper" two-story house, with cellar for canned goods, a full stove, glass windows, lidded slop jars to prevent the need to go to their outhouses at night and all the interior trimmings.

A house like Joshua's. The beds would have good cord supports for real stuffed mattresses and be four-posters. With four bedrooms upstairs, and a very large kitchen, dining room and parlor, it would be an excellent house! Raymond readily agreed and so they set to planning.

Robert watched his parents prepare a list of all the things needed for Big Jim's house. How happy God must be with two such generous and grand people.

He and Alfred had discussed both of their desires to marry within a year and Robert was pleased to hear his friend was putting down a "holding fee" on the Horn farm next to them, with the widow planning to move soon to Berryville with her sister it was ideal.

Even Carlie was better now. The shoulder much improved and although to his embarrassment, Mrs. Adams, still looked about the injury and insisted it have a protective bandage that she applied, it was all well and good. Carlie was happy now he had moved into the bunk house with the nine other men, four black and five white. All got along famously and assisted with reheating their food, bringing in water and so forth. No staffing troubles occurred.

The estate had no difficulties with the "Reconstruction" and the Yankee take over either. The Federal overseers attesting to the cooperation and help of the Adams didn't hurt and prevented any untoward intrusion by the new authorities. Thankfully all was good!

The following two weeks endured less upset and commotion than experienced so often lately, until a large carriage pulled up and Alfred Richards' family were seen alighting from the conveyance. They had been invited again and seemed very happy to come in their response this time. Mildred and the "girls" had been busy all week preparing for the visit with Mary having finished the third-floor rooms for them earlier.

Mildred had cautioned the dogs that it was "all right" so they were not growling nor did they have hackles up – but they were inspecting each visitor carefully. Mildred took the hands of the two youngest of the six children and led them to "meet" the dogs. The youngsters seemed alarmed but when Sasha, the female dog, rolled over to expose her belly for a rub, they all laughed and the children seemed to accept that the dogs, although as big as the two youngest children, were indeed friendly.

Alfred showed his family up to the third floor, helping carry some carpet bags and a suitcase.

"Al, my man, you are looking quite healthy and much better than I would have thought from the description of your injuries in your letters. How have you managed to get well so quickly?"

"Oh, Uncle, how can I ever explain how wonderful this family of Adams are? Mildred is so attentive to everyone's needs and has been the best nurse and caregiver I could have ever had – much superior to any tale I have heard from any hospital – north or south."

"Well, we are much in her debt then, for Gail and I didn't know if you would live or die from what you wrote of the devastation to your side and crawling around trying to survive the end of the war. How fortuitous you met Robert!"

"Well, we met at VMI and became friends instantly so we served in the war together. Helping avoid the onslaught of bullets from a much better armed northern army. We studied together – and "graduated", I guess, but had only a fraction of the training we would have had in peacetime. I expect a diploma but if I don't get one it won't matter, neither of us wanted to return there for more classes as were offered. I have put my money that you sent me from my bank down for the adjoining farm and plan to stay in this area. I also plan to marry shortly – as soon as the farmhouse is updated and my bride is ready. I will introduce you to her at dinner."

"Well, my Heavens! You certainly have it all planned out…and a prospective bride, too? How can you know so soon that you want to marry someone you hadn't even met until just a few months ago?"

"Oh, you will understand when you meet her! She is educated, knows how to do most everything on the estate – cooking, washing and canning. She sews and embroiders - wait until you meet her – she is just beautiful!" And he blushed a deep red.

"Well, I am anxious to do so…for you never seemed so interested in getting married before. I guess the war has matured you a lot. I understood from your letter that you intend to farm – I realize you just stated you put money on one. Are you certain it is what you want – you have been well educated to do a number of things…is farming really your desire?"

"It is indeed. I have no doubt. Up until coming here, I really did not know what I would do, just that it certainly wasn't to study law. But here I love seeing things grow and the Master and Missus here are such good examples of great people and a way to live. I can see myself being content with such a family and work a place like this for the rest of my life! And the Horn place is ideal."

He could tell that his Uncle wasn't convinced, but it didn't really matter. In time Uncle Tim would see and understand. His Uncle had no hold over him or his money – his parent's having trusted him enough to make their will explicit that he had the control. He had been amazed at the excellent condition of the whole place when he had toured it and put his deposit down. He felt he may paint the kitchen and the laundry porch but otherwise just move in furniture – well buy furniture and then move it in!

As the evening progressed and the many in the house sat down to a late supper in the dining room, it was pleasant getting acquainted. Both Mary and Julie were slated to be the mistresses of similar houses in the near future and would have a good example if they followed what they had seen done by Mildred – as the old folks or Amish would say – "For sure and certain!"

The End

Affluent farms were not unknown in this area during the 1800's but there were smaller – hand-to-mouth places too. However, everyone looked about the others and there was good cooperation among the residents. Not all were as considerate and giving as Mildred but there were some that went well out of their way to be helpful and look after the less fortunate or those suddenly ill or incapacitated in some manner. Even many small elementary schools were built and donated to the county by area residents – as both my great grandfather (the Lodge school) and my husband's great grandfather (the Dick school) had done.

The western portion of northern Virginia was a desirable place to live with farms and orchards enough to take care of the eating needs of most. Many of the owners of the various properties were in the southern military during the Civil War as were the more able-bodied sons. Some came home in good shape and some – like my great-grandfather were ill from being incarcerated in Yankee prisons or injured on the battlefields. While my relative lived considerable years after getting home, not all did and some were not enlisted as both Henry and Raymond in these first two stories.

VMI (Virginia Military Institute) recovered and continues to this day to be an excellent military school, with many graduate men of note, including: General George Marshall, Rear Admiral Richard E. Byrd, Marine Major General William Upshur and many others.

Book 3– A Foreigner In Their Midst

Chapter One

Gretchen Harper was very conscious that she wasn't "accepted" by all her neighbors. She spoke with a strong Dutch accent and was a "foreigner", but it didn't bother her a lot. She had expected worse treatment so was content. Several of the neighbors, in this lovely valley country area, were indeed helpful and friendly – like the newly wed Charlotte Thomas or the very energetic and "doer of good deeds", Mildred Adams.

She did wish her husband, Thomas Kennison Harper was home more. He had many business interests - the primary being a fleet of ships that he had carefully organized for their protection during the recent internal conflict this United States of America had endured called a "civil war". She personally felt there was little about it that was "civil"! So many dead! Most of that commotion was now at rest with just some trials and an occasional beggar or such. She would be forever grateful that his service had not been compulsory because of his fleet and therefore Thomas hadn't been forced to fight in the war. His ships were oft times required to deliver things but he was never incarcerated or such. His ships were endangered by theft or scuttling from pirates though but that had nothing to do with the war – just life in the 1800's.

When they had met, he had been a young college graduate "exploring" Europe on the financial back of well-to-do parents – also in the shipping business. She and Thomas were definitely not your normal couple. But my she loved him and he appeared to feel the same. They had married and come to the "states" and he had proceeded to get a fleet organized.

Right now, he was aboard one of the vessels bringing material for upholstery and clothes as well as much brass and silver from Europe, even some very lovely furniture and she and the three children were waiting with baited breath for his return.

When in the "states", his vessels were housed near Baltimore, Maryland - another state in this vast country. Her homeland of Holland was a fraction of the size and not nearly so complicated as to terrain and roads and orchards. Thinking about "home" made her somewhat sad. She missed the beautiful fields of tulips and other flowers, the windmills and the sound of the ocean when she used to visit her Aunt near the barriers that kept that same ocean from washing everything into it or maybe sucked out to it by the tremendous tides. But she was very glad she had married Thomas! She liked his name and was so glad he was pleased that she didn't abbreviate it to Tom or worse (according to him) Tommy. Her in-laws, who now lived in Maryland near the shore, were cordial – although obviously surprised when he brought home a "bride" and a foreign one at that. His mother was sometimes nice, always efficient and very busy – reminded her somewhat of Mildred Adams, but not as much generosity to the less fortunate as Mildred nor as generally friendly. Still, she was very active with helping her husband and his fleet and then doing some of the endless paperwork for Thomas as well. Quite well educated for a "lady" and seemed to be able to do the frequent manifests and invoices necessary for tracking cargo and the charges and receipts for the huge amount of money that exchanged hands.

Thomas had a full office staff and a man in charge of all cargo proofing and actions but the help of his mother was welcome when several ships were in port at once. He did not encourage Gretchen to help with any of that. With the three children and their farm to run, she was definitely busy enough, plus not near enough to Baltimore for day-to-day work. But she was certainly a "sounding board" for him as he would try to solve problems such as merchants who didn't pick up their orders, decisions on what to buy, or storm damage to a vessel and the occasional scuttling by thieves – not very frequent – not like two hundred years ago was experienced by others.

Only one small ship had been scuttled this year and the loss was not great. They were insured through an English company called Lloyds' of London, which had a long history of great service and prompt payment. Also, none of their sailors nor the Captain were hurt or retained for ransom by the thieves. So, the loss that did compute to them was definitely tolerable. They had missed some of their expected cargo due to the war but all told things were starting to shape up again. Of course, the war had only been over for a few months. Time would tell how successful they would be once this devastation was put to rest. Certainly, many in America, particularly in the south, would not have the wherewithal to purchase valuable imported goods like they did before this crushing war. But more were moving to business ventures rather than just farming.

Perhaps the ambitious businessmen would be interested in imports to help get their establishments' inventory off the ground. And northern citizens and companies were not affected like the southern ones, therefore they had orders coming in from Boston, New York, and Hartford to name a few. New York harbor was as busy as Baltimore but Thomas had agents that were promoting his goods in the north and they were amazingly successful. Therefore, he didn't need an actual office or the presence of vessels in that harbor.

Being in the business of goods transport, Thomas had discussed with her and his parents the advantage of the coming of railroads. Trains could carry much greater weight and at better speeds for land transport – opening up the growing west to their markets and goods sales. Plus, the construction of the tracks were increasing at a great rate – thus encouraging the movement of goods throughout the country with little regard for road repair and construction – except horse pulled wagons to and from the manufacturer arriving at the docks or at the railroad stations.

The businessmen could travel much more comfortably and quicker via the trains. The rumor among Robert's friends in the various transportation endeavors was that by year 1868, railroads would have newly designed "Pullman" cars for sleeping on long trips – actual berths with beds! It seemed unbelievable that also the transcontinental railroad that was started in 1863 would also be finished then – of course there may be delays – but the important people behind this effort were pushing greatly for it to be successful.

A completed rail system would be a great advantage to anyone in the shipping and manufacturing industries as amazing as it seems. Of course, hundreds of workers were being killed from various difficulties – some from the explosions of something called nitro glycerin that broke up rock formations in the way of the layout for building tracks. Or by other frequent accidents.

Another tragedy was that there were trains going both directions on the same track with no signal system and many passengers and workers were killed....no warnings could be given and schedules were not coordinated nor enough side-tracks available to rest a train that was in the way. But that was being designed, invented and tried – so hopefully they would either make tracks in opposite directions or sidetracks so trains could pass and with an improved teletype warning system. To Gretchen it sounded like the ones to make money were so anxious that they disregarded the dangers to their workers or the passengers – very unthinking of them!

Many names were bandied about: George Westinghouse – who was inventing and improving brakes; George Pullman the man behind the idea of the sleeping cars; and Jim Hill of the Great Northern Locomotives.

Thomas and his father had met these men as discussions increased but to Gretchen it sounded like a daydream. And so much at stake – the death toll would be enormous if they didn't manage to solve some of the issues like head-on collisions, buffalo on the tracks – which derailed the trains, robbers who boarded and stripped the passengers of their money and watches or jewels – then road off on horseback. Armed guards or officials seemed a partial solution for some of it to Gretchen but of course a woman's opinion wouldn't mean much. A few trains did have private guards paid for by the passengers or traveling merchants, to protect them or their wares. Such as bankers carrying gold or cash – maybe even jewels.

One other worry by some was the possibility of Indian attacks. While the antagonism between Indians and Whites was not severe right now – many who had forethought were worried. Both sides were concerned about the other and neither fully understood the objectives.

She had not heard much about the natives being an issue, however it was intrusion into territory they had hunted for years – wouldn't they be a problem? Indians called the trains "iron horses" and were leery of them, however she felt it only a small amount of time until problems arose with the natives!

She had to agree, as Thomas emphasized, IF it did work, the country would be well connected and their goods could reach all areas rapidly. Indians were slated to lose the most, of course, but it was at this time only partially a problem for the fledgling railroads. Stagecoaches and wagon trains were definitely too slow and dangerous and more subject to climate issues or small bands of marauding Indians. This rail system would be an advantage if the many problems could be worked out.

England had successful railroads in the early 1700's but the land was not strewn with so many obstacles or such tough terrain, nor Indians of course. Gretchen knew from listening to her husband's many discussions with other men in transportation of goods that the first North American "train" was called a 'gravity road' and built in 1764 for use during the Indian fighting and beginnings of military uses as portage at Niagara in Lewistown, New York. It was a fore binger of what was now being made and now they certainly were faster and could carry considerable weight of cargo.

My goodness she had spent too much of the morning daydreaming about trains and the shipping of their goods – Holy Cow as her friend Charlotte would say…the baby needed his milk again and to have his gruel plus she hadn't done a thing constructively in the kitchen. Helen, her oldest, had come to be "cleaned up" having obviously helped the man working in the garden again. At five she was an outdoor person for sure and certain – to capture an Amish phrase. The child could name almost all the plants – both vegetables and flowers – and loved spending every waking minute that she was allowed out of doors. Gretchen did insist she do lessons and with a good disposition it wasn't too difficult to get her to do so. Now Beatrice, "Bea", that was a different story! The child with the most bull-head of any Gretchen had ever met. At four, she made her wishes known as loudly as possible and although punished for it, didn't appear to improve with age. At least she would usually listen to the nanny, Harriet. Right now, she was coming with a large cookie in hand – knowing full well it was too close to luncheon time to eat it! Gretchen wondered how she had managed to sneak that under the very nose of Betty, the cook. Taking the remains of the cookie away, while ignoring the crying as a result, Gretchen washed Bea's face and hands and sent her to pick some flowers for the table. The frowning child, stating she would only do so if those great green worms were not on them, then left by the back door – not slamming it - Thank Heaven!

Gretchen picked up baby Thomas. What a boy! He would be at least his father's great height she felt certain. Of course, his grandfather on her side (her own father) was the tallest man in their community in Holland – and that was saying something as the nationality bred tall men.

The baby grinned at her and showed his two new teeth. She was well aware of them, having scars from where he took nourishment to prove it. She had made him some gruel and proceeded to feed him, which was interesting because being hungry all the time he could eat as fast as anyone could shovel it in his mouth! She remembered how thrilled his father had been when they had a boy. He loved his daughters to distraction, but something about having a son always seemed so important to men. Her father had been so proud of her brother Hans. He had turned out to be a tall and handsome man who worked with international shipping and so they got to see him on occasion when he came to the "states" to discuss the fleet and prospective cargo and things. He seemed delighted when Thomas had explained, recently, about the railroads.

There she was again thinking about trains – for Heaven's Sake!

Young Thomas (they had to come up with a nickname for the child) had finished the gruel in record order and she gave him a bottle of milk, hers almost dried up now. That didn't last long either! Then she gave him a cookie – the very flavor Bea had "stolen" and he gummed it and used the two new teeth as best he could. Every few minutes he would give her a grin that fore warned of the fact he would probably charm his way through life. She smiled back and remembered the first she had met "her" Thomas as he traveled through Holland on his graduation present from his parents – to see all of Europe that he could in a year. Well, she guessed she ruined that as soon as he gave her the same smile she had just seen on his son! As a result, he ended up staying in Holland after only three months of touring – which his mother made mention of on occasion. Gretchen didn't think for a minute that his mother seriously didn't like her but as Thomas' mother she felt or wanted to be in "control" and made quick work, in her inimitable way, to show it!

The baby was finished his cookie and fussed a little. She couldn't fill him up! Calling for Harriet to bring applesauce, she wiped his mouth of cookie crumbs and burped him. He again gave her "the grin" that would see him through anything and kicked his feet as he saw the applesauce bowl come. Applesauce had been new to Gretchen when she had arrived in Virginia but soon learned of its great value as a food for children and she herself liked it well enough that it was often on their table too. Apples were originally from Europe but none were grown in her part of Holland. Mildred Adams had shown her how adding things could make it a little different and still delicious – like raisins, cinnamon, dark sugar, nuts or so forth. Of course, for the baby – just plain apple sauce.

Finally, young Thomas, who burped again, nodded his head and went to sleep. She hugged him tightly as she took him to his crib. I think I will call him "Tom"; his father didn't like abbreviations but "Tom" seemed to suit a small boy just fine. My how she loved her children! It would be wonderful to have a couple more...not certain how Thomas would feel about that...but he may not mind. She really cared as deeply for Bea as the other two but hoped any more would have the easier personality. One Bea was enough per family.

Her duties were many and she didn't complain but seldom got to do anything she personally liked such as embroidery, music, or reading. She was busy every waking hour with the house, farm and three children. Particularly the farm took up a lot of time. Many crops and many employees made for considerable work.

Chapter Two

A little later that morning, as she got some upstairs things done like folding and putting away laundry, there was a squeal that could break glass. Gretchen hurried downstairs after checking Tom was resting and went to see what had Bea so excited...for it had to be her!

Thomas stood in the foyer holding his daughter who was kissing him and pulling his hair to hold on. "Bea, let up on my hair. You will make me bald and I'm looking old enough now!"

Looking at his beautiful wife, he said: "Hello, Love! I rode all night. I just couldn't stay away longer. Father wanted me to take a carriage but I knew I would make better time on Rider so came across country. Thankfully he didn't stumble into any gopher or groundhog holes! I caught the late-night ferry at Leesburg and here I am!"

Kissing him for all he was worth she said how wonderful it was that he had come. She had expected him back this week but hadn't dreamed he would be here this soon.

"Will that girl, the one Charlotte Thomas knows, be able to babysit this week? We could get away to a nice hotel in

Philadelphia and have another honeymoon."

"I don't know but I'll see her in a bit today and can ask. You have considerable mail so should we leave in two days? I oversaw the replanting of the two empty fields and hired help to do the corn – showing them how you like it done. They seemed agreeable. The chicken house has been increased at my request – poor things were on top of each other since we kept so many for egg hatchers recently. I had the devil of a time getting the chicken wire but Henry Thomas found it for me at the hardware in Middletown. Plus, the new female calves came from the man Henry recommended. They are very nice. They should enable us to increase the milk production quite well once they are fresh, then we will have some more of our own. I have had several requests for quantities of milk, it won't be hard to sell any extra, just like I have done with the eggs.. I am forever grateful that Henry is such a good friend and so very helpful.

Oh, I have gotten my new horse familiar with me. I can't wait to show you how my riding skills have improved. As you know I am still a little nervous in the saddle but we manage to work out almost every day and we are getting used to each other. You were correct that I can get about the farm much quicker than using a buggy. I imagine you would like to look the farm over a bit, too?"

"You took care of all that? And with the children into everything?" He inquired.

"Yup, I did indeed. Do I sound more like a Virginian when I say that?"

Laughing, he kissed her again and said she sounded just fine no matter what she said. As the light shown on her beautiful light blonde hair and with her rosy cheeks she was so very beautiful.

As the various staff finished preparing a late breakfast, Harriet took over caring for the three children, while Betty made certain the milk and eggs were put away. Gretchen and Thomas had a bit of late breakfast in the dining room – with peace and quiet, after he had held his son, who was again awake from the commotion. Then Thomas hugged and kissed Helen and hugged (while scolding) Bea who had taken her brother's cookie - again.

As he admonished his second daughter, he warned her that not too many years hence "young" Thomas would be able to defend himself. He believed the baby had grown inches in the two weeks he had been gone... the child was certainly going to be large!

"Remind me dear, if we go away, to let our part-time cook, know that baby Thomas is eating oatmeal, gruel and applesauce all ready. Betty knows of course but she is supposed to visit her mother the first of the week. I cannot keep your son fed on milk alone anymore."

"Just like Mother used to say about me as a youngster. She thought she would never get me filled up."

"Well, no wonder you have to duck to get in the doors…so you ate heartily too as a babe?"

"According to everything I've been told, I was always the tallest in my grade school classes too."

When they had finished breakfast and again played a bit with the girls, they headed to the barn for Thomas to look over the addition to the dairy herd. Oh, what great calves! So healthy and sturdy. Henry's recommendation was indeed fine…great stock. They were gentle and came slowly, hesitant to approach, and he pet them and talked to them in his very deep voice. Well, anyone could tell they liked that. As he moved on to look over the older cows and then go to the horse barn, the new calves bellowed as if to object that he was leaving them.

"My precious wife, how do you keep up with it all…staff seems to know so much, I realize you have been instructing them…but with three children, how do you do it?"

"Pshaw, no problem. I am well organized but you have hired so much help for me that I have lots of time. I don't read like I used to nor embroider much, but otherwise I get it all done. We could use another man in the barn now with these calves though – had really needed help before this. I do not muck stalls…isn't that the word they use here – muck?"

He laughed. "Yes "muck" is what is said. You are doing very well with our language. I am proud of you!" Thomas made mental note that his wife had given up two of her favorite things to care for their property and family. He was putting too much on her shoulders.

"Mildred and Charlotte help me by correcting if I say something wrong – after I let them know I wanted them to. And I listen well…it isn't hard. I am also trying to tone down my accent a little so it is easier for others to understand me. Now let's head back to the house and you can tell me what our ships are doing and how the cargo has come in. Have we lost any to scavengers lately? How are your parents? Do we have many contracts?"

"You are getting so much like Mother – in the business world anyway. Much sweeter personality, I am glad to say! My Dear, things are going well. All six ships finished their last runs without a single incident, the ones coming back here had to endure a doozy of a storm on the way back – but not to worry – nothing was lost and no one was hurt. Worst of it affected the ship Mary Belle and the Captain, as I am certain you will remember, is Roderick Anders. That man hasn't met a storm that can defeat him.   He can tell from the wind and velocity as well as the ocean direction of the currents how he has to avoid the worst and he manages quite well. Of course, he knows he will never be reprimanded for being late because of weather and that helps his decisions. He felt amused that one new hire was so sick, but the fellow will get 'sea legs' at some point."

"You are an excellent steward, Thomas. I believe better yet than your father, but please don't tell him I said that. He is just starting to like me after almost seven years!"

"Oh, he has come around quite well. He compliments you all the time. He even said he can see why I married you and that you are near perfect in every way. And don't take offence at his use of "near " because he has always thought he is the only perfect one…it must be trying on Mother!" Again, he laughed. He realized he was laughing a lot as he got home. His wonderful wife was the reason. He had indeed married "well". She understood things and worked hard and loved him better than he would have ever imagined a woman would for he was difficult, busy, and forgetful!

"Darling let's get the word out to Mildred and Raymond Adams, to Charlotte and James Thomas (including her father, Timothy Johnson) and others that we are looking for an excellent bull. If they have one for sale, we could easily own another but if not the loan of one would be helpful."

"How fortuitous! As I mentioned, Charlotte is to come by today for me to see to her embroidery. She is learning well but has trouble with the love knots and overstitch. I can give her the word and she can then tell the others. See it will be done right away!"

She had been busy clearing the table and when she looked up he had the most unusual expression on his face – sort of puzzled. "What have I done now? Did I use a wrong word? Why are you looking at me so?"

"Oh, you most certainly did not do anything wrong – but I am continually amazed how you get so much done! When do you have time to teach a friend to embroider? How can you be so very organized to invite someone here when you have three children, new animals, the farm books to keep, and acres of crops in the gathering stage. When I arrived, I saw Jason and he explained that you have them all scheduled already for harvesting the grain and replanting field number three! My Dear Wife, I am appalled at how much is doled out for you to do – yet you actually get it all done!"

She rushed over and kissed him soundly as she settled on his lap. "I am not overworked, if that is what you are saying. I have always been organized and the help we employ is beyond reproach. They understand and follow through on suggestions and instructions. If praise is needed it should go to them and not to me! When I mention something – they just DO it! I asked Mildred when she was here last week to see if she could gently inquire if I am too harsh or demanding. To find out what my staff thinks. But her later response was that they were all happy with me – just very glad I understand the whole operation and don't make mistakes that they would have to correct. Maybe they expected such…my being foreign is still a bit of puzzlement for them."

"I worry a lot about you, Dear. Are you really happy here so far away from your homeland?" He asked as he hugger her tighter.

"Oh, My Sweet Thomas! Do not worry about me. I am just fine. I would like to see Father and Aunt Marnie Nytham and so forth but I am all right! I have you and the children, I could not be happier! And my brother, Hans, gets to see us when he docks in America. Do not stress yourself about it. And I have made good friends - about two dozen or so – good people and generous to others. The kind of friends one would hope to make! See I am just fine." She said as he kissed her again and again and again.

They heard sobbing and looked down at Beatrice, who was genuinely crying.

"Oh, Poppet, come to Daddy. What is wrong? Why are your crying?"

"You kissed Momma so you are leaving again. I do not want you to leave again so soon!"

"Oh, Sweet Heavens! Bea, Daddy is not leaving again, yet. We just kissed because we love to kiss each other. We may take a trip in a couple days but not for long. Come here and sit on Daddy's lap."

As the little might crawled up on his lap, he was really happy. He hugged her and asked if she liked the doll he had sent? She started to cry again. "What is the matter now Bea? Did you not like the doll?"

"I, I, I took its head off and we can't fix her. I didn't mean to hurt her, really I didn't!"

Watching her husband, Gretchen thought she would choke from holding her breath to not laugh. Thomas' face was red likewise, but he got his composure back first and adjusted Beatrice more comfortably on his lap as Gretchen rose.

"I am sorry you broke your new doll, Poppet, but just like with babies such as your brother, they have to be handled nicely. You must have been too rough with her. I will look at the doll tonight after supper and see if she can be fixed.

But you must promise to be nicer with your toys from now on."

"Yes, Pappa. I will." And she jumped down and ran out of the room.

"Well, I don't mean to call your younger daughter a liar, but if she keeps that promise I will write it in the bible – for she is a terror of the worst order! Thankfully she hasn't hurt Tom but I don't trust her alone with him - she is liable to feed him a beef bone or chicken meal…she uses no sense at all!"

Thomas couldn't help but laugh again. It wasn't funny and he imagined his younger daughter was a constant headache to his wife, but her spirit was such fun!

It was then he remembered he had a gift for his wife. "Sweetheart, come with me while I empty my saddle bags, if you have time that is."

"Of course, I do…anything to be with you! I miss you so when you are gone!"

Taking a heavily wrapped package out of one side of the bags on the porch floor, Thomas handed it to Gretchen.

"What is this? It is quite heavy and wrapped to withstand the wars. What have you bought?"

"Well, open it and see. It is just a little present for my beautiful wife. I do hope you like it!"

Gently removing the heavy wrappings including a pretty scarf as the last covering, there was a gorgeous large bowl of Delft porcelain. "Oh, Thomas! You remembered how I looked at this when we were first stepping out. How could you with all your busy schedule and many work problems have remembered? I am thrilled. Here let's put it immediately on the sideboard in the dining room so the children cannot knock it over. Oh, I am so happy." And she kissed him, many times.

"Well, I guess I should buy porcelain more often! Although you never ration your kisses I must admit. Do you really like it so well?"

"I really do and had planned to paint this room – now I know exactly the color blue to use. It will be hard to get it properly mixed in town but if we go to Philadelphia I imagine there will be a greater selection of colors. I am certain I will be able to know which is correct, for I have looked at and admired such porcelain all my days. However, to be certain I will take the pepper mill that Hans gave me, which is also Delft. Thank you again love!"

Luncheon was a bit of a circus. Both girls were invited to eat with the adults and amazing as it may be, Bea was quiet and ate without disrupting anything, probably sobered by actually being allowed to eat in the dining room.

It was going to be a very busy day....as they finished luncheon a little late because of a lot of talking and catching up, Charlotte arrived accompanied by James. Well, that was nice – it would give Thomas company while Gretchen studied the skill of Charlotte's stitches and had some "woman gossip". True to her expectations, the men headed to look over the calves and the barn situation and discuss the hiring of someone else to assist Thomas' wife with some of the many barn duties. Someone of good sense and long experience would be perfect.

Chapter Three

After Thomas explained the type of farm employee he was looking for, James said he didn't want to change Thomas' mind but he would recommend a young man he knew quite well, just out of school. Someone as good as Joshua would be ideal and this boy seemed to have the same work ethic. He was quite smart and wanted to continue with farm work as he had done since just a 'pup', his father having worked for Charlotte's parents all his life. The boy was really good with horses, even able to break young ones. He also could handle cattle, including helping with birthing and knowing how to skillfully handle bulls – even cantankerous ones! His name is Raymond (he likes Ray) Dyke and he is very reliable.

Thomas appeared to give it some thought but decided he would indeed interview the boy – well really a man now if he was finished school. Thomas wondered why he had even hesitated, when everything James said fit into exactly what they needed – then he realized he was jealous! JEALOUS? Really? Well, he believed he was. After all his wife was indeed a blonde beauty and he, himself, was away from home a lot. Not that he didn't trust Gretchen – of course he did...but a handsome young man working all the time?

Then he had to laugh at himself. For Heaven's sake, get her the best help he could. If that was a nice young man, then so be it. But he knew in his heart of hearts he was still uneasy. Never in his born days had he needed to even think of such things. He had been very satisfactory looking, well-built, and tall since before his teens. Women were always interested in him – but never had he been stirred to chase after any and had rarely dated growing up, not even in college…but that was before Holland. He could still remember that day he was walking through Rotterdam and seen the beautiful, statuesque woman also walking along the road. She was unaccompanied and he wondered if she was married – although she looked quite young. He sped up his walk and approached her, quickly deciding to ask if there was somewhere nearby to get some lunch. With a heavy accent but perfect English, she had said her favorite place was a couple blocks over, would he like her to lead the way? Well, tarnation he would indeed – but he simply said: "Yes, that would be nice."

As he was reminiscing, he realized James had been talking to him. "I'm so sorry, I was miles away. What do you think of my heifers?"

"I was just stating that you were lucky, or rather your wife was, to purchase them when she did because several others wanted them also. They have excellent breeding and there is a history of great milk production in their lineage. My Dad had just gotten a couple from the same diary and is very pleased with their health. We'll see how much milk they give next year after they have calves.

"Well, if Henry approves then they must be nice indeed." Commented Thomas. When the guys were going back to the house, Joshua came and told them two men had been seen loitering near the far barn. It currently didn't have any animals or tools of any great value in it but it seemed strange for unknown men to be in that area.

Thomas called for his horse while James got on his and they immediately rode that way to look things over. Of course, it wasn't unheard of for stray people to be looking for work but such would not have been at an unused barn – instead coming to the regular barn or even the back door of the house to beg for work or food. Something wasn't right!

They hadn't requested staff to out ride, but two of the men had and almost caught up with them just as they divided and Thomas went to the front of the "empty" barn and James to the back. Both Riley and Tim were now close enough to soon be of help. At that moment there was a shot fired and Thomas fell off his horse and a man rode out of the barn on a horse with no saddle.

James shouted to Tim to circle and protect Thomas while he rode like the wind with his hunting rifle pulled from its saddle holster. James hadn't been in the confederate army for nothing! He soon got close enough to the man to fire – and fire he did! The man literally flew off his horse onto the ground and was writhing in pain. Behind him he heard another shot and looked over his shoulder. Evidently Tim had also succeeded in hitting the second culprit, who was trying to get away as well, this time on foot.

There was no catching the unsaddled horse for it had taken off like the very devil was riding it – headed in the general direction of the Adams farm – probably stolen from them or a neighbor of theirs.

Turning his mount on a six pence, James headed back toward where Thomas lay still on the ground. Oh, please Dear Lord do not let him be seriously hurt! Such a wonderful man and the father of three children...please save him, Lord, he prayed.

Back at the house, several had heard the shots, although not close but definitely on their property to carry the sound to the house. Two more of the men were saddling and ready to ride in the general direction of the spare barn.

Both Charlotte and Gretchen were alarmed as Charlotte got on her horse at the hitching post by the door and staff were ordered to bring Mistress Harper's. Gretchen gave orders for the children to be watched and not allowed outside. Lock all doors except the kitchen exit. She had grabbed her derringer from the sideboard drawer. She was an excellent shot, never having held a gun until she married but wanting, in her inimitable way, to know how things work. Charlotte had a gun in her saddle bag and being agile was able to extract it as she rode. They were within sight of the old barn when Gretchen gave a cry and galloped her horse up to where she saw Thomas on the ground.

There was so much blood! She wasn't familiar with people being shot and bleeding, but knew in her heart that this was way, way an excessive amount of blood! Evidently Thomas had been shot at point blank range and thankfully it appeared to be more shoulder than chest but dear God above the blood! She called for a wagon and horse immediately.

She was assured that one of their men had ridden for the doctor. Kneeling beside her husband she began tearing at the clothes to expose the actual injury. James handed her his short knife – nice and sharp, and it cut through the material better. As she tried to straightened out Thomas' arm, he groaned. Well, she didn't want to hurt him but was very glad to hear him make a noise! She asked for one of the fellows to loan her their canteen and she took off her petticoat, using the knife to help she tore it to pieces. One of the workers went to get more water and she used all in the canteen to wash his face, neck, and wrists to cool him off. Using James short knife, she could cut away clothes and make bandages out of some of her petticoat until they could get to whatever clean cloth was found at the house. It was hard to bandage a shoulder but she managed to stuff the wound with enough pressure to stem the bleeding.

She called for one of the men to bring a wagon with a bed of straw and a large blanket or comforter - quickly please. He was to leave word at the kitchen door for clean towels, soap, water, and any antiseptic they could find to be readied but not come with it – they would bring Thomas back to the house.

Suddenly, remembering Thomas' horse, she asked if they had found it and Jason replied they had and Tim had ridden it back to the stable. She then asked after the two crooks who had done such damage. Johnson replied that one was dead and the other shot, but not life threatening. He was tied up with their belts until the sheriff came.

Gretchen sent Charlotte back to the house to prepare the bed in the master room with extra blanket and sheets to protect the mattress and a table set up with anything she felt may be needed to nurse such a wound, knowing Charlotte had nursed James when he got home from the war.

As the wagon bed was prepared with straw for padding as comfortably as possible, she asked the men to very carefully lift Thomas onto the straw that they had thoughtfully covered with a quilt someone had raced to obtain from the nearby workers' house. She had James assist her up onto the wagon beside her husband, where she kissed him and began talking in a soft voice. It wasn't long before he opened his eyes and looked confused. She immediately told him what was happening and that he would be all right but had a shot to the shoulder. "It looks like the mini-ball went through the flesh. I don't believe it is lodged in your arm, Dear. That is good news – less chance of infection. Now lay as still as you can. I will hold your head and stay close so you will rock as little as possible while we get you back to the house."

He muttered he understood and grimaced with pain. She lay beside him holding his neck and with her one hand under his injured shoulder - resting his head. This put her mouth right against his ear and she whispered: "Thomas, Dear, you must get well quickly, because I will need you most urgently in a few months. I am pregnant again, Dear. Now does that help you heal?"

His eyes flew open and he looked into hers. Then of all things, he laughed...actually laughed. Then let out a "Whoop!" which made his friend and staff wonder what in the world could make him do so when he was so very injured. "Well, you certainly have a way to make me forget I was shot, My Love! I am very pleased. I would not have asked you for another child or more with three already but I am very happy. I would indeed like a brood. OUCH! Do they have to hit every hole in the field?"

As they got to the back door of the house, Charles and Edward lifted Thomas to remove him from the wagon but it was lucky that the Mistress and James were handy too – for they almost dropped his great weight and length. Staff assured them the bed was turned back, bandages, soap, hot water, and tea as well as pain medicine were all awaiting them upstairs. They made it through the kitchen and rested a minute before tackling the long staircase to the second floor. Finally, he was in bed. Not quite settled properly but he helped as he could and Gretchen as well lifted his legs – albeit with great difficulty.

He was getting his breath back when he heard a sob and looking down from the high bed, there sat Bea in the corner of his room crying. Beside her, trying the best to console her sister also sat Helen, with red eyes as well.

"Oh, girls, do not cry for me, please. Daddy will be all right. I am injured and you must not touch my bad shoulder but I will get well. I am certain you will help your mother nurse me – won't you?" Coming immediately to the side of the bed both girls said they would help nurse him. What should they do?

"Well, right now, I suggest you go and have your luncheon, if you haven't already. I am very tired and hurt a good bit. They have sent for the doctor and until he is finished, I would like to rest quietly, but you go now and eat. I will send for you a little later. Can you do that for Pappa?" Both nodded solemnly and left the room, passing their Mother on the way.

"How did they get in here? I would have sworn they were in the kitchen with cookies and milk." "They wanted to nurse me they said, I can just imagine how that would have gone...but isn't it dear that they care so much! I told them we would send for them after the doctor has gone....maybe that will delay their interest a while."

"I guess the only other time they have seen either of us laid up was when I gave birth to Tom and at their age, they won't remember that so very well."

"Are you really with child again, or did I dream that?" "Oh, you didn't dream it...I feel certain I am for my stomach is all sixes and sevens today...of course my husband being shot hasn't helped any!" and she gave him the smile he so liked.

Hearing a booming voice and heavy tread, Thomas got prepared for great discomfort, as Doctor Weems came up the stairs. "What have you gotten yourself into now, Thomas?" Said the booming voice. "Well, I really didn't get INTO anything. I was shot before I even got a look at the men trespassing in my back barn. I am certain if they hadn't been discovered by some of my men, they would have been most disappointed because there is nothing of value in that barn at present – just broken tools and two extra wagon wheels. I will say though the fellow is a pretty good shot – oops WAS a pretty good shot, for I understand from Charles that the one killed is the one who shot me. The other is being held until the sheriff arrives. I am not at all concerned if he is uncomfortable! While I am known to not have much of a temper, I believe my good graces are at an end – at least for the next few days. Are you going to make me more miserable now?"

Laughing and nodding his head in the affirmative, the good doctor proceeded to remove the bandage Gretchen had applied and looked and poked and prodded until Thomas was not at all certain he could keep his composure any longer. Goodness gracious did that HURT!

"Lean forward Thomas, bend as far as you can toward your knees…I must look as I can and see what damage there is. The shot went all the way through it looks like, which is excellent for I won't have to dig for the bullet, you wouldn't enjoy that if I had to. I have some distilled alcohol from my bag to clean it – you may want to bite on the covers – this will hurt – I mean really hurt!" Well, that wasn't a lie – hurt it did! Gretchen was helping and had used a couple towels to catch the extra liquid so his bed wasn't getting soaked. She made soothing noises like she did to the baby when he cried. It almost made Thomas laugh – almost, for Doctor Weems was now sewing up the muscles and then the skin. Thomas didn't cry out nor pass out but it was the most pain he had ever been in.

At least an hour later, the doctor said he was finished. "Nice clean shot you had there. Very nice. Not too much damage. Sorry I hurt you but you handled it well. Now take some laudanum, drink some liquids and nap all you can. You are most fortunate that no bone was broken and the bullet was not in it. Most fortunate! It will hurt even more tomorrow, I imagine, but keep a good attitude and I am certain your wife will attend you well. I smelled roasted chicken in your kitchen and hope to beg a bit of luncheon. If you feel like eating, you can, but don't try it if you think you are nauseous because that will disturb your shoulder.

I'll be back in a few days but send a rider for me if you have a problem. Don't try to pick up the children, ride your horse or do anything strenuous…I don't want to have to resew that gash! Good day Thomas. Good day, Gretchen." And they heard him whistling as he went downstairs.

"Well, I guess if I sewed people up all the time I would be as nonchalant as that but my goodness, he acted like it was nothing at all!"

"Yes, Dear Heart, he did indeed. I am sorry I groaned so but it really hurt like the very devil! Do you think there is any soup in the kitchen? I am hungry but not at all certain of my stomach…maybe some soup?"

"I know Lois planned some but the day has not exactly gone the right way. I'll see what I can rustle up for you. There is most likely soup because the children like it including the baby who can have at least the broth – I'll bring whatever I find that I think you can eat. Do you want to see any of the men? I imagine they are waiting for news of you."

"By all means, send them up. Once I am asleep then you can have visitors and the children leave me alone, but I don't mind some company now. And soup or gravy and bread would be very nice. Thank you, Darling! And I am so sorry about our trip to Philadelphia – I will make time to take you when I am better. If you would, please write to my parents about my little set back and that if possible they should check the manifests from my ships – or hire that part-time man, Andreas, to come and work for a bit…that would be good. He is Greek but speaks better English than I, and knows all about invoices."

"I'll write to them immediately, Dear. Now you rest until your meal comes up. I'll check on the children and be certain they have been fed. I myself do not feel much like eating – between this crisis and the pregnancy, I am off my feed, as the saying goes."

"Please, Dear, try to eat something – soup or fruit salad – something. And thank you, Love, for all your attention."

Going downstairs she realized she had a terrible knot in her chest – anxiety probably. Her husband shot! For goodness sake, what next! She wasn't at all sorry the one man was dead, for he was the one who had shot Thomas. Awful of her, probably, but true none the less. Now to fix Thomas a nice tray and be certain the children had eaten. She hadn't heard a peep out of the baby so someone was probably spoiling him. The girls were subdued, the shooting had been a terrible awakening for them – their Father was never out of action and to see him hurt would stay with them, she thought.

Later, after sending a man with the letter to Thomas' parents, she was pleased to see he ate biscuits with gravy and applesauce. Nice mix of easy to digest foods. He didn't complain but was very pale and she knew he must hurt a good deal. She gave him a dose of laudanum, wiped his face with a warm and wet cloth, and straighten his covers just as he went to sleep.

Later she had to encourage the "girls" to not try to open his door and disturb him but promised to let them know as soon as he awoke.

Thomas slept through most of the afternoon and into night with her helping him drink some wine and making soothing noises as she would turn his pillow to the cool side or wipe his brow. All told not a bad night for the first since he was so badly hurt.

Chapter Four

Days flew by and it had been over a week since the intrusion of the men in the back barn and Thomas' shot in the shoulder. He was still in considerable pain, poor soul! Any movement bothered the wound and even with pillows to keep the shoulder from touching the bed, he was discomforted. She had peeked regularly at the wound, careful to reattach the bandage, but the stitching looked all right. No yellowing, excessive swelling or oozing and so forth. He wasn't taking any laudanum now – at his insistence, but he also wasn't sleeping well because of the discomfort and the inability to lie on his right side like he preferred. Gretchen would still climb in and snuggle on his "good" side – she couldn't resist.

As to her health, she was just fine and as pregnant as could be. She thought about writing to his parents with her news, she had let them know about Thomas, but decided to let it ride a while. When she wrote she had assured them he was doing very well and she thanked them for getting help for his people at the docks, as he had requested.

Just after lunch, she looked up from her farm records as Bea let out a squeal and said her Grammy and Pap were here. Here? My goodness they had come all this way. Well, if Thomas was her son she would probably have done the same. She hurriedly fixed her hair, washed her face, and went downstairs.

Standing in the foyer, looking like a storm cloud was none other than Thomas' mother. "Gretchen, what in the world has happened? Was the information I got correct, he has been shot! Actually shot?"

Fleetingly Thomas' wife wondered at his Mother's comment since the information was from her so of course he had indeed been shot, but she didn't say anything. Her mother-in-law was a force to be reconned with – so ignoring her was the smart way to go. She nodded the affirmative to his father.

"How about I take you up to see him? He will be so pleased to see you both. Then we will get you settled in the largest spare room and give you some refreshments. Come up this way." And Gretchen walked toward the stairs.

"Wait, I need to fix my hair. I don't want him to see me so disheveled! I have not seen him in ages and ages!"

Out of the mouths of babes – in her frank and open way, Helen said: "But Grammy he was just in Baltimore last week!"

Thomas' wife was very proud of herself when she didn't laugh or say something sarcastic. "Come Mr. and Mrs. Harper, I will take you up. He will be so pleased!" She knew she was repeating herself but it was safer territory than correcting what the woman had said.

"Well, I guess I can although I don't look like myself at all…such a trip and in such hurry – very havey skavey!"

Thomas' wife would have liked to have told her she didn't HAVE to come, but wisely kept her mouth closed.

When the bedroom door opened, Thomas tried to rise and smooth his hair with his one good hand. "Mother, is that you? Dad, come in, come in! You didn't need to travel all this way…I am getting excellent care and feeling much better today."

Gretchen was putting two chairs by the bed for them and saying she would go down and get refreshments. However, Betty had already come up behind the group with a tray of tea and biscuits, so his wife instead went to the other side of the bed and supported Thomas with several pillows and a rolled quilt so he could lean back on his good shoulder then she moved to stand behind the guests.

"What have you gotten yourself into now, Thomas. Out here in the hinterlands – what in the world have you done!" Demanded his mother in an unpleasant voice.

Before he could answer, his father told her to "be still" and "leave the boy alone" and "couldn't she see he was hurt for Heaven's sake?"

Thomas looked across at his wife who stood behind her in-laws and she winked! Now she was really having trouble to keep from laughing. Thomas said: "Dear, won't you have some of this tea? Staff have provided enough cups and the large tea pot."

"Thank you, Sweetheart, but I will wait and have something in a bit. You all enjoy your visit and you can explain to your Mother how the shooting occurred. I'll go check on Tom and then the girls. Plus, I'll need to help staff get a larger dinner ready. I will return very soon. Do you need anything, Dear?"

"No, Sweetheart, this tea and biscuits will be just fine. I look forward to whatever you have staff prepare for dinner. I am quite hungry after my nap and look forward to something else to eat. I believe I will try to make it downstairs to the dining room, please have staff set me a place."

"Oh, that is fine! The girls will be so pleased to see you downstairs. But be careful of that shoulder, although it looked like it was healing properly when I cleaned it this morning – still be careful! And don't try to get dressed, which would entail moving the shoulder a lot – just put on that beautiful robe your mother gave you last Christmas. I will help feed Tom and then assist with adding more food to the dinner being prepared. We will see you shortly. Please ask your Father to assist you by walking in front of you as I do – we don't want a fall to add to your problems."

She wanted to chuckle but didn't. The "robe" in question had not been worn because he felt it was too elaborate and not a color he liked but she guessed he would have to wear it today.

The next two hours was taken up with trying to get enough food into young Tom to satisfy his hunger and then feeding the girls, who would be allowed to eat dessert at the table with the adults – IF they behaved…good luck with that! Helen would be all right but Bea - anybody's guess.

Gretchen then realized she still had on the soiled dress she had worn all day. Assuring Betty didn't need her, she high-tailed it up to her dressing room to change and do something with the pile of blonde hair that insisted on falling into her face. Wearing the blue dress with cream lace that Thomas liked best, she put her mother's combs in her hair and added a clean lacy apron. She would "do" she guessed. Of course, his Mother would find fault with something but hard to tell what!

When she got back downstairs, she was alarmed that Thomas looked so white. He must be in considerable pain – although man-like he wouldn't admit it.

"Thomas – go back to bed! You look awful. I will bring your dinner if no one else will. Now! Go!" Said his mother in a voice heard all through the house.

"I will do no such thing! I am eating at the table tonight. I am fine. Of course, I am pale I have not been outside for almost a couple weeks. Do not give me orders in my own home."

Bea rushed up and took his hand. "Here Papa I will walk you in for dinner. We ate ours in the kitchen but we can have dessert with you. Will you have dessert, Papa?"

"Oh, I love dessert. Yes and to eat it with my girls will be very nice. Do you know what dessert we are having or is it a secret?"

"It's a secret, but we helped Nancy make it. I even added some of the ap.... Uh I can't say but I helped." Trying not to laugh he changed the subject but was looking forward to apple pie! Feeling sorry for his wife, he tried to make good conversation with his mother. He hated the way the woman always treated Gretchen. He had indeed "married well" and it made him angry when anyone treated her less than perfect...for she was perfect!

His father rose, expecting to pull out his chair probably but little Bea had it all taken care of. "That's a fine helper you have there, Son. Isn't she alert. And so grown up. I know it hasn't been a long time since I saw the children but they certainly are progressing well."

"Much credit is due to Gretchen. She instructs them well and keeps them busy learning new things, including cooking and animal care. Both are learning to read and do their numbers as well as help others. Helen has started embroidery too. Just big stitches for now, but she is really quite accomplished already."

"How does your wife ever have the time? You are gone so much and such a huge estate to run, I can't imagine she would have time for the children and the household!" Exclaimed his Mother.

"She is a wonder and I am forever conscious that she does not have enough time to relax and just read or do needlepoint or something. But she insists it is all fine – of course she is very organized and extremely smart. That helps considerably I am certain. By the way did you bring the last invoices from the three ships that should have made port this week?"

"How did you remember that? With a bullet hole in your shoulder, three children and this big property – I think you would relish the opportunity to forget Baltimore entirely." His mother exclaimed.

"Of course, I would not forget my shipping business, Mother! Did you bring the papers?"

"I tried not to but your Father insisted. They are in my reticule. They haven't put any food on the table, I'll run up and get them now while we talk about it. Your men did a great job of finding the things you wanted and your brother-in-law provided much help in locating the china and silver items. You really picked some lovely things that should sell very well in Boston and New York."

"You mean you talked to Hans, so he is in Baltimore? Why in the name of heavens didn't you bring him with you when you came here?"

"I offered, Son, but he said he would look after all the things you had to be delivered and the things from his ship as well. He is really quite capable isn't he? Very smart and understands shipping."

"Of course, he does Dad. He has been doing it for years and years. He is very successful as were his father and uncle.

You always seem surprised but they have been in the business longer than our family and more successful too! I think you forget how accomplished they are." Said Thomas with authority.

He noticed his Mother frown, but thankfully she didn't say anything for he would have taken her to task had it not been complimentary toward Hans.

Dinner went reasonably well, given his Mother found fault with too much salt in the cured ham, beans not cooked as she liked, and fruit salad served with the meal instead of with dessert. She was really stretching to find things to complain about. Thomas wondered how his father had put up with her bad attitude all these years.

How it happened Thomas didn't know, but the girls seemed to sense the tension and acted very grown-up and polite. Bea insisted on serving her father his apple pie with custard sauce and then offered to serve her grandmother. It was hard to tell who was the most surprised among the adults, but wonder of wonders, Grandma

Harper said she would love for Bea to serve her and gave the child a big smile. She may not know it but she moved up several steps in the good graces of both Gretchen and Thomas.

Thomas was pleased that he had eaten almost everything and still felt quite well. A sign he was indeed "on the mend" as Dr. Weems was known to say. The girls had joined the adults in the dining room for dessert and there were no "issues" – Bea was definitely on her good behavior. As supper was finished, three of the adults went to the study and Gretchen excused herself to see to young Tom and assist kitchen staff with the clean-up, so very glad she had an excuse to avoid her mother-in-law when she could.

As they had some port and discussed the various cargo and where it was likely to sell the best, Charles came in to check on Thomas and ask if there were any instructions for the next day. Thomas' mother was sniffing at discussion of "farm business", Thomas informed her the farm was more profitable than the imports. Both parents were obviously very surprised – never having run a farm in their lives. Thomas explained that the overhead was so much less than ships, insurance and crews – even with the many farm workers and that with Gretchen in charge they successfully raised many plants, animals, and by products for very good revenue indeed. He bragged on his wife and her good management – saying the import business would improve if he could just spare her – but he definitely could not and with a fourth child on the way she was needed right here at home.

As Charles got his instructions for the next day, Gretchen returned with raspberry cordial and a plate of cookies, followed by the girls in their nightdresses and wishing to say a "proper" good evening to their grandparents. Both Thomas and Gretchen were delighted that the grandparents seemed so nice with the children – even Grandma let down her abrupt ways and hugged and kissed, each wishing the girls "Sweet Dreams".

Well, the evening was ending on a good note anyway. Thomas took the opportunity to say he would walk the girls up to their bedroom and turn in himself. He wasn't ill but was very tried.

The next two days were similar with Thomas interacting with his parents and the three of them taking note of the hundred or so things Gretchen had to do. It was alarming how the woman could work!

Finally, Thomas' parents packed up and left to return to Baltimore – saying they needed to "see to" things there after five days. Gretchen knew they had made progress – his mother not being nearly so critical as when they came – but it was still a trying time having them visit.

Chapter Five

The next three days were at least better with the grandmother not being there to be so judgmental and Thomas much improved. He made a daily trip to the barn, let Helen show him the garden that she loved to tend, and took both girls by the hand to the stable to "meet" the horses. That daily event would usually tire him out and he would nap before lunch, but everyone could see he was in less pain and a better color – not so drawn and white. Sometimes his father or mother, before they left, had taken a tour of the farm and found they were learning a lot about the workings of it and how busy their daughter-in-law was. When they would complement her, she was thunder struck but finally realized it wasn't havey skavey but actual pride they were taking in all she accomplished and the work involved – not to mention the good revenue generated.

Of course, this trip to the barn encouraged both girls to want to learn to ride. The third night, after the girls' interest in horses started, he and Gretchen decided two ponies were in order. None of their full-grown horses had a gentle enough mouth for the girls to be able to handle and ponies would be easier for staff to walk along and keep a hold of horse and rider. It was made VERY clear to both girls that only good behavior would be considered and any acting out or doing anything not previously approved of by their parents or staff would mean they would NOT ride for two weeks...the other girl being allowed to continue if she did not misbehave.

Gretchen immediately wrote a note to Charlotte requesting a recommendation of a stable that may have ponies and would let them bring the girls for "trial" rides. The very next day, a messenger from the Thomas farm came and stated they had a well-trained pony, fairly old and gentle and would let the girls come and get used to riding at their convenience, they even had a child-sized saddle. Charlotte also said in her note that her father, Timothy Johnson, had two ponies on her home estate that could be borrowed if the experimental rides at the Thomas farm were successful enough to warrant some "real" lessons. Charlotte also added that her father would have given them the ponies but she was with child and they would be kept for her own children to ride. May goodness! Wasn't that wonderful news. Charlotte and James would be such wonderful parents and she could just see Henry spoiling a grandchild! Gretchen sent a congratulatory note on the pregnancy and said she would be glad to be any help as needed.

Gretchen thought: Once more in her life, she was amazed by the caring of the locals – Charlotte in particular, but others as well. She was so very happy here. She missed Thomas terribly when he was in Baltimore or at sea running the import business but she would not move to a city area for anything. Here is where the children needed to be. She immediately sent a message back by Jason that they would love to try a ride – would it suit for them to come in two days? Jason was to wait for the response. She never mentioned it to the girls but did tell Thomas as he gingerly came into the kitchen for a late breakfast. He had tried riding yesterday – against her wishes –

and it had taken a serious toll on his shoulder. Nothing looked too angry in the area of the wound – but still obviously too soon. She gave him a few mild exercises to do and hoped it would work out the pain and strengthen the shoulder – nothing too drastic – they didn't want it to start to bleed again!

The girls were unusually quiet lately and went about their "duties" such as flowers (without large green worms) and the garden. She wondered if they might like a dog. She had grown up with a dog and they are great protection and fun too. She would check with Thomas about that when he came back in from talking to the men about the fall plans.

She was just getting started on some paperwork regarding sales of produce and piglets when staff answered the door and a deputy sheriff was there. What now?

"Mrs. Harper? I am Deputy John Williams. I need to find out what occurred two weeks ago when your husband was shot and subsequently a prospective robber as well. We have interviewed the man captured and believe he tells the truth on things but in order to close my file on the case, I need to speak with your husband and anyone else who can explain what happened."

"I will be more than glad to help you, Sir. However, I believe you should indeed talk to my husband, Thomas. He is in the horse barn, which is the first of the three toward the back and west of the house. Would you like me to send someone to get him or will you go there?"

"I will go to him. I am pleased he is up and about. I was not at all certain he would be able to do any work."

"He isn't able to do much but he can oversee and discuss issues with staff. He is still quite injured, as you will see from his large bandage. I will accompany you. Please walk around to the back door and I will join you as soon as I make certain staff are watching the baby."

As the deputy headed to the back door he could hear giggles of little girls from somewhere in the direction of the three barns. What a huge farm they had here. And so well taken care of from appearances anyway. Over on the next ridge he could see a barn in need of a little repair and no staff around. That must be the place the two men had trespassed. From the pleasant woman he had just met and from what he had heard about Thomas Harper, they would have most likely been given work and food – had they asked instead of being criminals…well they got it coming. Now, unfortunately, he had to help clean up the paperwork.

He had seen Thomas Harper out and about since the man had bought the Templeton farm several years ago but had not met the wife. From what he saw at the front door she was a real beauty. A bit of an accent but pleasant, well-spoken and quite lovely. Thomas had done well for himself in getting such a great farm and evidently also in a pretty wife. The man could work, he'd say that for him. Running a multi-ship import company in Baltimore and this great farm. A lot of animals and about 10 fields of various crops…yup, he'd done all right for himself. I wonder if the wife helps, she speaks as if she is well educated. This would be an interesting interview.

He heard children giggle and about that time Thomas came out of a barn with two little girls…beauties both of them – very similar to their mother. This must mean they have three children since the wife had mentioned a baby. Wow, they were certainly busy. Good thing Thomas hadn't been killed; she would have had her hands full then!

Seeing a strange man coming toward them, both girls came to a halt and reached for their father's hands. "Helen and Beatrice, this is Deputy Williams. He is a sergeant and probably going to ask me some questions about the shooting. Can you both go to the kitchen, please. Tell Betty you are to have cookies and whatever you want to drink – tell her I said so. Now go…both of you. Send your mother out if she can leave your brother, Tom. Oh, never mind, here she comes now. Both of you go – straight to the kitchen and do not come back to the barn until I say – Okay?"

"Yes, Papa." They said in unison.

"Good afternoon, Mr. Harper. As I told your wife, I have been sent to fill out some paperwork on the set to you had just over two weeks ago. The judge is going to announce a trial date now the one felon that is left seems better and I must get some information. I am sorry to bother you Sir."

"It is not a problem. I was prepared to come to your office, when the Doctor will allow but since you are here, let's get it done now. Come with me to the house – we will use the front door rather than go through the kitchen. Gretchen, Dear, you come too please. You were in on part of it and probably know more about my injuries than I do."

The girls had disappeared into the kitchen and Betty had waved so they could do their adult conversation in private.

"Sheriff, I can refer you to Doctor Weems for the extent of Thomas' injury. He was shot through the shoulder and thankfully there were enough of staff handy and I had come just after the shots were fired. Thomas, raise your shirt please so he can see the extent of the bandage. The shot, thankfully, went completely through the shoulder and did not break any bones…making the healing much easier and the doctor did not have to "dig" to retrieve the bullet. But it was quite a bad injury and now, at two weeks he is just able to be up and about the farm. But of course, still has considerable difficulty and pain nor can he do any lifting, riding or activity that would move the arm. Doctor Weems has not released him to do any work either on the farm or to return to Baltimore to see to our import business." Said Gretchen.

"Oh, Dear, that is quite an extensive bandage. I am so sorry for the difficulty and pain you have suffered. I can give testimony if this goes to trial that I have seen the area shot and it is quite serious –

both entry and exit. Now I have some questions – just routine, but answer as you can please:

"Thomas had you ever seen or employed the men involved in your injury?"

"Not to my knowledge, Sheriff. I am most certain I haven't employed either man but have not inquired of staff if they have been here before to appeal for work. But if so they would usually be referred to me or my wife. Gretchen, have you seen either before?"

"No, I have not, Dear."

"About what I would have thought. That type is looking for "easy" ways and not usually interested in real work. I am so sorry you had the intrusion and such injury. Now, do I have permission to contact Doctor Weems – just a formality – trying to prevent this going to court and requiring you to appear."

"Oh, you may do whatever you need. It is fine to ask the good doctor anything you may need to know. He is quite articulate and I can just imagine what he would say in a courtroom…the criminal would not be pleased I can almost guarantee." And Thomas laughed.

"Well, I think that should cover what I need. I have verified you were shot and have witnesses and also the trespassing on your property. We should be fine. I will probably also inquire of Dr. Weems if he would care to testify. He will probably not be subpoenaed but it would be a nice witness to have."

"Deputy Williams, John, wouldn't you like some luncheon? Staff should have put the finishing touches to it while we have talked, there is always enough for one more."

"Well, if I am not imposing, I would love some lunch. I have two other stops before I can go back to the station. Are you certain I will not interfere with your family plans?"

"No, the girls ate a large and late breakfast, so they are being allowed cookies with milk and I had just finished feeding young Tom when you arrived.

Here is the wash basin in this little room and the dining room is the next door up."

Quickly setting an extra place, Gretchen smiled and kissed her husband. "I hope you don't mind, Dear, but the poor man's stomach rumbled and I felt certain he must be hungry. We have baked chicken and dressing today – so it will be a nice meal for him."

"You really are on top of things aren't you? How do you manage? I can hardly get around to just see to things and know you are doing much more. Really, do you not need more help?"

"Oh, pshaw, I am just fine. If we do hire for the barn as we have discussed that would be marvelous, for I sometimes help there but it takes me away from Tom and the girls more – so let's just say barn help will be forthcoming and that should take care of it! You may not realize but I did find a woman who used to work full time that will now come if we entertain and for holidays or when your parents come and so forth. I understand from Madeline that she is a wonder in the kitchen and can bake or cook as well as set up tables, decorate and generally organize. As the children get bigger and with another small baby, she would come in very handy."

"Let's get her straight away. You need to rest more now that you are pregnant right behind Tom. You do too much and I worry. Then maybe you can embroider again or just take an afternoon to have tea with friends."

"All right. If you are sure. Here's John. Our meal will be ready soon, let's go into the dining room and have a beverage. Tell us about your family, John. Do you have children?"

"I have two boys – about half grown. I have been looking for a suitable farm with good instruction and owners I like. Would you need any help from young men here?"

"How fortuitous! We do indeed. Some of the work will be hard, because it will entail gathering crops soon, but the rest of the year would not be as bad. Now I don't want them to give up school at all.

It must be understood, if they work, they still do their studies. I know that is your call but I am a firm believer in education and cannot in all honesty hire a young person away from their schoolwork."

"That is perfect! I do not want them to stop school either. Suppose I bring them over this Saturday. Would that work in your schedule?"

"It would indeed. I am not going back to Baltimore for four weeks or so yet – per the doctor – so will have ample time to show them what I will need. We are also planning on putting in some new orchard too. Our trees are getting old for they were on the property when we bought it and although kept properly pruned, they do not produce well anymore. The boys would be perfect to help with that in the spring. And here comes our luncheon…right on time. What would you like to drink?"

Chapter Six

Nothing alarming occurred in the ensuing next few weeks. A man was seen again in the vicinity of the old barn. But he left when two of Thomas' men approached and they didn't follow him or pay much attention. There weren't the stragglers like there had been immediately after the civil war and they just figured he was looking for mischief but didn't pursue him when he left as soon as he saw the workers, he did not appear to be armed.

The following couple weeks flew by and Thomas improved almost daily. Once the big bandage was removed there were only two small ones – one at the exit wound on the back and a smaller one yet at his front shoulder. He was getting information regularly from Baltimore and had actually made a trip for five days (counting travel) the week before – leaving Gretchen home to "worry herself silly". Thankfully he had taken the carriage and a driver and not tried to ride his horse the whole way.

Baby Thomas was actually walking now…not too steadily but getting places and staff had to be careful to put chairs in from of the iron stove so he wouldn't burn his little hands and the dog and cats were learning to flee when they saw him approach. For he adored them but the feeling was not returned.

On Thomas' arrival back home, he was really his "old self" and was riding horses, even exercising a new one, and doing chores and playing with the children without incident. No one thought to mention the sighting of a man near the old barn again and in truth had really forgotten it. Knowing he had two ships arriving in Baltimore in four days' time, he made another trip that direction – kissing Gretchen and the children and insisting he was just fine to be on Rider. It left Gretchen to handle all estate business and she was starting to get a little uncomfortable with the newest baby evident in her stomach. But it was only when she had to lean over much but otherwise had no pregnancy difficulties. Young Tom was crawling everywhere, and even taking a few shaky steps, while they all had to be certain to not step on him. His sisters were taking pony lessons with great regularity and a used piano had been bought so music lessons were taking up some of their time as well.

Gretchen missed Thomas, as she always did when he wasn't close, but imports were doing really well now and he felt he should take advantage of the market while "the iron was hot" as the new saying goes.

On the very day he arrived back, Sheriff John Williams came again with another deputy. He asked to speak to both Thomas and Gretchen. They ushered him into the parlor and instructed staff to increase the amount of food for lunch and be prepared to serve in an hour.

"I apologize for bothering you both but something has occurred that you need to know. It appears the men that were in your old barn were indeed planning something far worse than trespassing or a little theft. They had been hired by a "gentleman" (I use the word advisedly) who wanted Thomas dead. The idea being that Gretchen, as a woman even though the spouse, could not inherit and with her having no male heirs of legitimate age, who are citizens, the person, hiring the men to kill Thomas, would succeed in causing the property to be put up for sale. This person then thinking it could be purchased easily at auction for a bargain price.

The sheriff continued to explain: "Not many people would have the money to buy such an estate because of the war. Evidently they did not know about Thomas' parents living in Baltimore, who could run this and any inheritance that may be achieved. It does not appear they are cognizant of any will Thomas may have on record with the local Clerk of the Court, either. Maybe hesitant to show their hand. If you do not have such a will naming a male heir of age, I suggest you do so to protect Gretchen. With women having little rights and no apparent man/relative of age to inherit – thus a sale - and most likely at well less than the property is worth. While your parents may qualify, it would be best to have something in writing from you.

It is further believed the plotter had planned to kill the men who would shoot Thomas so there were no witnesses to the plot. A court would have had difficulty but would not have awarded the property to such a person if his plan was known. The usual result would have been to award the property to your parents – should they appear and request to do so. But inheritance cases are a mess in the courts right now with so many laws changing since the war is over. It would be much safer, legally, to actually name a male heir such as your own father.

Before the war between the states, 23 of the states had legislated for women's rights – most allowing inheritance or purchase of property. As you may know, Virginia, North Carolina and South Carolina are now arguing the passing of such laws in their assemblies, such would allow women ownership or inheritance of property like this…but the fellow was evidently not up on the legislation <u>or</u> trying to get under the date it is to pass."

As the poor man stopped to draw breath, Gretchen was beside herself. They would have killed Thomas to steal this farm? Had she really heard that correctly? Oh, Dear God!

Thomas, always knowing her thoughts, came and hugged her tightly. "You know don't you that it would NOT have been taken. My parents would have seen to that. I know Mother isn't an easy person but she is extremely fair and being a businesswoman is quite supportive of any woman owning property. When here she was very, very complimentary of you and even this past week has mentioned on several occasions of how you have single-handedly brought this farm into a successful and profitable state."

"Oh, Thomas, to think you may have been killed because of ME! I cannot countenance it. I really can't. Thank you Deputy Williams. We will gladly testify as needed and take precautions to preserve the property rights as we would wish and for the children's benefit."

As if to ease the situation, all three children came into the room, clamoring for their lunch, with Tom being carried almost upside down by his older sister. He had learned to walk very, very early but his sisters liked to carry him. He was not fusing in the least, however, and grinned at the deputy. He was such an outgoing. pleasant child and seemed to like everyone. Gretchen asked if Betty had lunch ready and all three children nodded that she did.

"Come Sheriff and your deputy too, there will be plenty to share. We will feed you some lunch before you have to continue on with your duties. And I thank you so much for coming and giving us such good information. I certainly hope the man in question, who is apparently behind it, is arrested for his part in the attempt on Thomas!"

Thomas showed the law enforcement men where to wash up and the children went to eat in the kitchen. Finally, the adults all found seats around the dining room table. Each seemed to purposely avoid any more of the conversation about the inheritance and the set-to at the old barn. Local news and a discussion of the Dutch stew recipe took up most of the time. The stew was very well accepted and was a favorite with Thomas because it had his wife's homemade noodles in it and the chicken just fell from the bones in a delicious array of gravy and vegetables fresh from their garden.

Once the deputies had gone on their way, Thomas immediately wrote to his parents and also his solicitor. They would take care of this estate title immediately. Even if there was new legislation, they would just have to change it in a few months again should legislation pass that would allow Beatrice to inherit. No sense in taking any chances. Being shot had shown him how vulnerable he was and he must take great care of his family.

In the late afternoon, Thomas went to tell the men about the sheriff's information and to be extra watchful. He also suggested they see if one or two deputy sheriffs wouldn't like to earn a little extra money and work part-time at the estate, keeping their guns and holsters in plain sight and knowing how to watch for culprits who may be up to no good. Having the agreement of the men, he decided to ride Gretchen's horse since she couldn't now and the fellow was prancing his feet in pleasure.

Gretchen was doing some knitting, making a new cover for her upcoming baby and thinking seriously about the problems at hand. The nanny had all three children busy with the girls practicing their reading out loud and Tom down for his nap. She was drawn from her revere when there was a commotion at the front door. Almost immediately she knew who it was. For the Dutch accent was plain and the booming laugh as well. Sure, enough Hans Nytham had been directed to where she was in the library. Her wonderful brother, so extremely tall and handsome was coming down the hall.

"I apologize for coming unannounced but got finished my peddling of porcelain and silver plus some mahogany furniture in the Capitol – so I thought I'd pay my favorite sister a visit."

"Favorite sister my foot – your only sister! Oh, how glad I am to see you! How are things at home? Is father well, is your business still so very successful, is the old windmill still that vivid blue that Charlene painted it? I have started painting again and thought to reproduce it but no one would believe it was really that color."

"Oh, God, I have missed you so...and your sense of humor. I don't want to speak ill of your in-laws but I don't believe they have a sense of humor at all. I try but get nowhere with my jokes. They are very nice though and so cooperative. We help each other at the docks and with deliveries of goods. Yes, the windmill is still a vivid blue. Where are the children? I must see your brood! I cannot believe you have three little mites!"

"Well, you better sit down for I have to tell you, I have a fourth on the way! You and Ingrid better get busy for I have quite a start on you! You are still engaged to Ingrid are you not?"

"I am and one reason for my stop is to tell you we plan to marry in March. Is there any way you could come? I would so love for you and Thomas to be there."

"Oh, Dear, I guess not. My new baby will be so tiny and still on breast milk. I do not think a long ocean voyage would be possible and I just couldn't leave the children at home...no way! Why don't you make a trip to the States as your honeymoon? We could have a nice party here and you could show her the country. Would that work?"

"I had promised to bring her "sometime", so maybe that would be possible. I'll check my shipping log for that time. I had purposely not engaged too much in order to have time with her but maybe she would like to come along! As we first started dating I was quite smitten but she is not a good sailor and so I hesitated. But

I have taken her out on the water more and now she is doing much better, let me think on it – I'll let you know. I should be back in the states in six weeks and we can talk more about it then."

A whirlwind came through the door and then stopped abruptly. Both Helen and Bea stood amazed in the entrance, dragging Tom with them. Tom gave Hans a serious look and then struggled to get out of his sisters' hold – each had an arm. As they let him go, he staggered but quickly got his footing – quite a feat for such a small boy – then he immediately ran (well, staggered) to Hans with his arms up. Everyone was amazed. He, of course, had never met the huge man before but was not the least bit shy.

In his deep baritone, Hans said: "Well, you must be Tom. How nice to see you! Here, let me put you on my shoulders – mind you don't bump your head on the ceiling!"

"Hans, be careful, I do believe he is touching his head. You better sit down with him."

Bea, of all people, started to cry. "Why is that man holding Tom? He can't have him, Tom is MINE!"

"Oh, Bea, I will not take your brother. Come here. Dear. Don't you remember me? I am your uncle Hans. I am your Mama's brother. Here, come sit beside me on the settee. How are you, Helen? You certainly remember me don't you?"

"Oh, yes, you are the chocolate man! I remember. You came with Father from the big ships and you brought us chocolates!"

"I did indeed and if you go to my saddle bags, I believe you will find some more chocolates!" Helen immediately left the room and Bea cried some more.

As the chocolates arrived in the hands of Helen, Bea settled down – amazing what a large box of candy can do!

"Don't eat but two each. You will have supper very soon. I know your Father will be hungry and this great fellow can eat more than your father ever thought of doing!"

Helen looked at him inquisitively and asked could he really eat more than Pappa?

"Well, I believe I may be able to – particularly today since I missed lunch to come and see my sister and her beautiful children. And also, her husband of course."

The neat Helen had eaten both of her candies without a problem but Gretchen was hurrying to Bea before she wiped her hands on her new dress.

"Whose horse is out front? I don't recall seeing it before. Gretchen, where are you?"

Hans had put his finger to his lips and stepped behind the door. Both girls got the giggles and his wife had to hold her son to keep him from spoiling things.

As Thomas entered the room – Hans jumped out at him and everyone laughed but Bea who started to cry again. What in tarnation had gotten into the girl, none of them could figure.

After a quick explanation, Thomas picked Bea up and asked what the problem was. Sobbing she said: "That man may take Tom. He gave us candy but I don't want him to take my 'bruder'."

"Oh, he won't take him. Hans is too lazy to change diapers and I doubt he knows how. Do not worry about it – why don't you go and sit on his head – that will keep him quiet!"

Finally, Bea laughed at the thought of sitting on the strange man's head. Just to show her how funny it was Hans picked up baby Tom and set him in his blonde curls. "Look how high your brother is now." Said Hans. "Wouldn't you like to be as high as the ceiling too, Bea?" Shaking her head "no" she backed up but Helen was quick to pick up on the game and stood in front of her uncle with her hands up. When seated in the blonde curls she giggled but then the dinner bell rang and Hans had to lift her down for she definitely was close to hitting the ceiling as he stood up. He went to get his bag off the horse while his sister asked Helen to get the men to put the great beast up for the night.

The children were promised dessert with the adults and sent off to the kitchen.

Dinner was served and as conversation started Gretchen told her brother of their difficulties with the man hiring someone to kill Thomas so the estate could be purchased.

"Of all the idiotic things! Your parents told me of your injury but nothing about an attempt on your life intentionally. They – well we – assumed it was just to steal things. You mean your laws would allow him to take the estate away from you, Gretchen?"

"Sort of, it would be put up for sale if there was no male heir. The reasoning behind his attempt we believe, is that it would bring less than it is worth at a quick sale. Therefore, he would obtain an excellent property at a bargain. Now some of the states have laws allowing the woman to inherit but not all and

Virginia's law is not finalized yet, at least as we understand it from the Sheriff. I need to get in touch with my parents, post-haste and be certain Father is willing to be my heir. I had written but should maybe act even quicker than originally planned We can then redraw the titling if or when the law changes and Gretchen can inherit it all with the added condition should we both die that it go in trust for the children....in other words so no one else will get it."

"What utter nonsense! But I guess it is necessary if you are correct about such strange laws. My sister has worked every bit as hard as you and it should be ascertained that she has the property in such an awful event as your demise. And it is quite antiquated for the law to not recognize the wife as heir. But you say that is changing...about time!" Said Hans with a frown. "I am certain you have written to your parents or will but I can also talk to them. I must leave early in the morning to return to Baltimore because my ship is slated to sail with the tide very late tomorrow night. In case your parents want to immediately leave for here to get the paperwork on record, I will offer my agent to assist Andreas with any issues while they are in Virginia."

"Thank you, Hans. That is a very good idea. First thing in the morning I will arm myself and take one of my men and go into Winchester and to my attorney for the paperwork to begin if he hasn't. I will explain the need for quick action and get a change in title on record as soon as possible. As Gretchen and I discussed, it can easily be changed back once we are certain legislation has passed and is not being challenged."

"I will be seeing you again before very long, my wares were so well received that I will have a ship load to bring to the states within a few weeks of my return to Holland. I am doing very well in South America and the islands. I sell a lot to France and Germany – of course shipped by land travel in most cases. This was a most profitable trip and looks like it will bring me some regular customers in America."

"I am so glad. My imports of china, jewels, tapestry, cloth – such as velvet, and furniture are successful also as are my parents'. With the influx of gold from the mine in Georgia that was discovered in 1820 and with the recent excitement in California at Sutter's Mill from 1848 to 1855 including other mines, everyone in Europe is clamoring for all kinds of gold objects, jewelry and religious statues or alter ornamentations. Then I bring back furniture and frames and other carvings on the return. It is working out quite well, but I will be selling two of my ships. If you know someone in the market, I plan to sell the "Belle" and the "Night Hawk" as soon as I am offered a goodly price. I am running myself to death and now with four children I should be at home more. I WANT to be at home more!"

"Well, good gracious, I will take the Night Hawk off your hands. I was going to look for an additional ship on my return home but assume you will not overcharge your own brother-in-law. Can we work up a contract and price tonight?"

"Yes, indeed we can! I will not overcharge you either. Gretchen, what do you think dear? You have been awfully quiet over there – is all this agreeable with you?"

"Oh, Dear Goodness! Of course, it is. To have you home more is worth giving up anything! And not only am I pleased but the children will be ecstatic! Not to brag but I have not shown you the farm books in some time. I was going to when you got home two times ago but then you got yourself shot and this last time was such a rush, we haven't discussed business much expect some farm issues…I am not certain you realize how much money I have made here at home. We will discuss it more tonight, but it exceeds any two of your ships!"

"You are kidding, aren't you, Sister? That you have made that much money growing vegetables and raising animals? Surely you jest!" Said Hans.

"No, I am not joking you. With the added cows and the increased chicken houses and having now plowed up the three previously unused fields and replanted fruit trees, by next year I should see another 20% increase in <u>profits,</u> conservatively. At current prices it would be 32%! Now do you "gentlemen" see what I do besides birthing children?" And she laughed.

Neither man could say a thing and Gretchen realized she would need to note this in her journal – she actually had the two speechless – well first time for everything!

THE END

Farms were profitable when skillfully handled and with the war over money was slowly becoming more available. Those willing to work were finally seeing good results. Two things that affected commerce that were "unusual" were the influx of gold and the railroads. Plus of course, the end of the civil war allowed for those energies to go to more humane purposes such as the beginning of a lot of manufacturing and reconstruction in the south. The north too was now able to use resources for better purposes than outfitting an army. It wouldn't be until World War I that military action would take so much of the resources – with the brief Spanish-American War (less than six months of 1898) not being too serious a drain on things.